A Real Friend

A Real Friend
© 2007 by Melanie L. Wilber
Revised and Updated, 2014
All Rights Reserved

This is a work of fiction. The characters, incidents, and dialogues are products of the author's imagination. Except for well-known historical and contemporary figures, any resemblance to actual events or persons is entirely coincidental.

Dedication

*For all of the real friends I've had;
I'm so thankful for you*

A friend loves at all times.

Proverbs 17:17

Chapter One

It was after eight o'clock p.m. by the time Brianne's dad pulled into the driveway of her grandparents' home in Bellingham, Washington. Brianne felt tired and ready to get out and stretch her legs. She loved her family, but after five hours in the van, reading her sister all of her books several times, and J.T. and Jeffrey going stir-crazy in the seat behind her for the last hour, her patience had reached its limit.

The only one who didn't appear travel-weary was her brother Steven. He was going to be turning nine next month, but he loved traveling. One of the positive aspects of his mild autism was his ability to remember things, including specific details about ways to get places and all the things they would see along the way. While his brothers were busy with their video games and trying to play-wrestle in the back seat of the van, Steven was quietly looking out the window, making random announcements about significant landmarks, like the McDonald's with a particularly great play-place they had stopped at before, and rest stops he remembered with automatic flushing toilets: he was afraid of them, so they avoided them whenever possible.

Getting out of the van in front of their grandparents' country home, ten miles outside the northern Washington city, Steven appeared ready to begin the day, not end it like the rest of them. And Brianne had to smile as he exuberantly ran up the front steps to ring the doorbell—a job that was exclusively his every time they came here.

They left their things in the van for now. It hadn't been decided for sure, but her mom and dad and brothers would probably be staying at a nearby motel for tonight. Her mom's younger sisters and their families had already arrived yesterday and would be staying through Christmas Day. Her grandparents' home was large, but it had its limits, and four families was one too many.

She and Beth would be staying here in a small bedroom they usually shared with two of her cousins, if Beth would agree to stay without Mommy here too. When they'd been here for Thanksgiving last year, Beth hadn't wanted to, but she was a year older now and had lost some of her need to be around Mommy all the time.

Stepping inside the house, Brianne took in the familiar sights and smells of the older home and was facing many relatives within seconds. Her mom's younger sisters, Aunt Julie and Aunt Kathy, were both married and had four kids each. Aunt Julie had twin daughters who were Brianne's age—just two months older, and two boys who were nine and six. Aunt Kathy had two boys and two girls who were all younger than her.

Brianne said 'hi' to everyone and gave hugs all around, but seeing Jenna and Justine was particularly enjoyable. Her twin cousins, who were not at all identical, had become good friends to her over the years, even though they usually only saw each other twice a year. Jenna had blonde hair she wore at shoulder-length, and Justine had brown hair she wore long—halfway down her back. Their facial features were more similar, and they looked a lot like her aunt, especially the older they got, but Jenna was her height, and Justine was several inches shorter.

Seeing her grandparents again was also sweet and satisfying. Grandma Anne was a spunky, petite woman with graying-blonde hair who loved to play board games, take pictures of her grandchildren, and talk about the latest ways she had seen God's love and blessings in her life. And Grandpa Lewis was a tall and slender man with a soft-spoken, gentle nature who loved to tease and share good stories. He was a writer who had a series of children's fantasy books published in the 1970s and 80s, and he'd had countless articles and short-stories published in magazines. He was currently writing another series of children's books, two of which were published already, and he also worked as a writer and editor for the *Bellingham Gazette*, a local community newspaper that came out twice a week.

Brianne had read all of his books when she was younger, and she had read some of them to Jeffrey before he learned to read well. She wanted to start reading them to Beth soon, but she didn't think her sister was ready to understand them yet. Brianne had read them all again last year for herself, and whenever she had to do a book report for school, she almost always used one of her grandpa's books.

"How are you, peanut?" he asked, giving her a loving hug. He'd always called her that for as long as she could remember. She had been born a month early and had been so small, weighing only five pounds.

"I'm good," she said. "But I think you should start calling me asparagus soon."

"I can see that," he said, laying his palm on top of her head and measuring to where she came on his chest. "Whoo-eee. You're going to be about six feet, aren't you?"

She laughed. "Maybe not that tall."

"Hard to say with a grandmother who's barely 5'2", but a grandfather who's 6'2"."

"I know. How does that happen? How does Grandma even kiss you?"

He lifted her off the ground and kissed her on the forehead. "Something like that," he said.

She laughed and stepped over to hug her grandmother next who had already greeted her brothers. Beth was still in her mom's arms, taking all of this in. It took her awhile to warm up in a new environment.

"How are you, honey?" her grandmother said. Brianne had been at eye level with her this summer, but now she wasn't.

"Taller," she said, and they both laughed.

"How have you been with your friend moving away?" she asked sincerely.

"Okay. It's been hard, but God is taking good care of me."

"He always does when we trust Him to, and even when we don't."

"I brought the DVD of our school play," she said, knowing her grandparents had been hoping to see it.

"Oh, good. I can't wait."

After hanging around and talking to everyone for a few minutes, her aunts started putting their younger ones to bed, and her mom said it was time to go over to the motel.

"I think we'll take Beth with us for tonight, honey," her mom said, holding a sleepy-eyed Beth against her. "Maybe tomorrow she'll be ready to stay here, but I don't think it's worth trying tonight."

"Can I stay here?"

"Absolutely. And I think we'll have J.T stay too. He can sleep on the couch in the den. Just keep an eye on him for me, will you?"

"Sure. When should he go to bed?"

"Whenever the other boys do. And you don't stay up too late, okay?"

"That might be more up to Jenna and Justine than me."

"I know. Do the best you can."

Brianne went out to get her bags and her pillow, and she took them upstairs to the bedroom at the end of the hall. It was the smallest upstairs room, but it also had the best view of the water. Brianne thought it was beautiful here, only a few miles south of the Canadian Border, and there had always been a desire in her heart to possibly live here someday.

Brianne set her things on the double bed beside the window. Jenna and Justine would be sleeping on the bunk beds, and they had their stuff strewn all over the place. One noticeable difference in her cousins from when she'd seen them in June was they both suddenly seemed very into their looks, and seeing the makeup bags, nail polish, and fashionable clothes lying all over the beds and littering the floor, she felt like she had this summer when she'd gone to camp and seen similar scenes on the bunks of her cabin mates.

"Hey, Brianne," Jenna said as they both came into the room.

"Hi," she said, taking things out of her bag she wanted to put in the bathroom down the hall so she wouldn't have to constantly be digging around them to get to her clothes.

Justine climbed onto the top bunk, and Jenna plopped onto the bottom one. Brianne noticed they had on matching pants, sort of. Jenna's were blue and Justine's were lavender, but the sweat pants both had words across the bottoms. Jenna's said, "Super Cute", and Justine's said, "Let's Dance".

That was one style of clothing her parents would not allow her to wear, and she honestly didn't want to. Partly because she always felt weird looking at some girl's butt and reading the words; and partly because of something Austin had told her this summer. They were at camp, and she and Sarah were walking with him after they went swimming. There were two girls walking in front of them who had pants on like that, and Sarah had said, "Why don't they just wear a sign that says, "Please look at my butt."? And Austin said, "But don't let me catch you looking, or I'll turn you in for harassment."

They had both looked at him. Brianne felt surprised by his comment, and Sarah had asked him why he said that, and he told them.

"That happened to Michael. We were walking down the hall, and he just said the words that were right in front of us, but she turned him in. He had to go talk to Principal Ruiz and the school counselor. They gave him a warning but told him the next time he would get suspended."

Brianne tried not to have judgmental thoughts about her cousins, but she could see this visit and her time with them was going to be different than it ever had before. And with as much as she wanted to be here visiting her grandparents and having time with Jenna and Justine too, she suddenly felt lonely for Sarah, and for Austin.

Okay, Jesus. Help me to be content and not be wishing I was back home or that I could have spent one of these weeks with Sarah.

Jenna and Justine peppered her with questions for the next fifteen minutes, wanting to know what her seventh-grade year had been like so far, what guys she liked, and what things she had done outside of school.

When they asked if she had a boyfriend, she said, "I have several guys as friends, but not like that."

She decided against telling them about what had happened with Ashlee and Silas, but she did say she had a new neighbor who was her age.

"What's he like?" Jenna asked. "Is he cute?"

"Yes. And he's really nice. His dad is a pastor too, so that helped us to connect easily. And he has an older sister who—"

Jenna interrupted her. "You've *connected* with him, huh? He sounds like more than a friend to me."

"Yeah," Justine added. "It sounds like a boy-friend."

Jenna and Justine laughed, and Brianne felt like she was in the middle of a cheesy teen movie. What had happened to her cousins? They were acting more like Ashlee than the girls she had always liked spending time with.

"I prefer the term, guy-friend," she said. "That way people don't get the wrong idea."

"You should ask him out," Jenna said matter-of-factly.

Brianne decided right then she wasn't going to mention Silas or Austin again. She knew if her cousins found out she had gone to Pizza Playhouse with Silas and to the movies with Austin, they would say she didn't have just one "boy-friend", but two!

Chapter Two

Brianne waited anxiously for her mom and dad to arrive at her grandparents' house on Monday morning. Jenna and Justine were still sleeping, but she had gotten up early. When she saw the van coming up the driveway from the front window in the living room, she waited for them to come inside, but she felt like running out and telling them she wanted to go home.

"How did you sleep?" her mom asked, giving her a good-morning hug inside the front door.

"I'll tell you later," she said, not hiding her subdued mood.

"Everything okay?" her mom asked, appearing concerned.

"Not really," she said, holding back the tears.

Her mother didn't brush her words aside. "You boys go see what Grandma's got going for breakfast," she said to Steven and Jeffrey. "Jacob, can you take Beth?"

Her dad took Beth into his arms and stepped away with her brothers. Her mom led the way outside and told her to come along. Brianne followed and they went to the van because it was about ten degrees below zero out. Her mom got in on the driver's side, and she went around to the front passenger door.

"What happened?" her mom asked once they were inside.

Brianne decided to be honest. Her night had been unbelievable. "Jenna and Justine are so different. It's like having two Ashlees to deal with at once!"

"When did you go to bed?"

"It wasn't that late, but they kept talking until like two a.m., and they kept twisting everything I said. I finally stopped talking and they just talked to each other, and it wasn't good, Mom. I didn't know what to say."

"What did they talk about?"

"I'm not sure I should tell you. I think they'll feel like I'm tattling on them."

"Could they get hurt, or hurt someone else?"

Brianne wasn't sure. "Yeah, maybe."

"Tell me, Bree. I'll decide if it's worth mentioning."

"To who? Their mom and dad?"

"Maybe. They're my nieces, Brianne. I care about them."

Brianne told her what she could remember—the stuff that concerned her the most. Jenna had a boyfriend her mom and dad didn't know about. Originally she said she didn't have one because her parents didn't want her to, but then later Justine let it slip. Jenna had been sneaking out to go to the movies with him. Justine and Jenna would go to a friend's house to spend the night, and then Jenna's boyfriend would come pick her up from there. He was an eighth grader, and he had a brother who was seventeen who was willing to take them wherever he was going with his girlfriend—usually to the movies or a party. One time she hadn't come back to their friend's house until one a.m.

Her mom listened to the things about Jenna and then asked, "Anything else?"

"I think Justine has some friends who aren't a good influence on her: the friend who covers for Jenna and some others. And I'm not sure, but I think Justine might be trying to lose weight in an unhealthy way."

"Throwing up, you mean?"

"Yes."

"Why do you think that?"

"Jenna said something about being hungry around midnight, and Justine said, 'I can't even think about eating too much while we're here', and then Jenna said, 'How much weight have you gained since Friday?', and Justine said, 'Three pounds.' I don't have any friends who notice when they've gained three pounds in two days, and that's one of the things I've heard to listen for when we've learned about eating disorders in health class."

Her mom nodded. "You're probably right."

"Are you going to say anything?"

"I think I have to." Her mom thought for a moment. "I might wait until after they go home though. This probably isn't the right time or place. I'll talk to your dad and see what he thinks."

Brianne let the tears fall then. She had been wondering what to do all night, and she was worried about what her cousins would think if she told anyone, and yet she knew she had done the right thing.

Her mom held her and reassured her of that. "I'm proud of you, sweetheart. Thanks for telling me. If they say anything else, let me know, but I'll take it from here. You just be the best cousin to them you know how to be. Don't be afraid to tell them what you think, but don't feel like you have to either."

"Can I stay at the motel with you tonight? I think I only slept for two hours."

"Yes. I don't think Beth is going to be ready to sleep here tonight yet either. Grandma wanted to have the boys stay in the trailer with her and Grandpa one night. I think that will have to be tonight."

They went inside and had breakfast. Brianne didn't see her cousins until ten-thirty when they finally came downstairs. She tried to act normal around them, but it was hard. And not just because of what they told her last night, but because they were so different. Different from her. Different than they used to be.

She spent most of the day with Beth and her younger cousins. Her grandparents had a closet full of board games and puzzles, and she played *Candy Land, Hi-Ho! Cherry-O, Sorry,* and *Pretty Pretty Princess* over and over. When Jenna and Justine wanted to go shopping in the afternoon and asked if she wanted to go, she said no.

"You could use my phone to call your boyfriend," Jenna said. "It has unlimited talk and texting."

"He's not my boyfriend," she said. "And if I wanted to call him, I'd just ask my dad if I could use his."

"Okay, suit yourself," Jenna said.

After they were gone, she did go ask her dad if she could use his phone to call Sarah. She had wanted to while she was here anyway and had planned to tomorrow or on Christmas Day, but she could use a good talk with her best friend right now.

He said it was fine, and she took it upstairs to the bedroom to make the call. But Sarah wasn't at home and she didn't answer her cell phone either, so she decided to call Austin instead, not knowing if she would tell him about her interesting night or not, but after some initial small-talk, she told him a brief version.

"Not quite the vacation you were expecting?"

"No. Do you think I did the right thing?"

"Telling your mom?"

"Yes."

"Definitely, Brianne. That's a no-brainer."

That made her feel better. "Okay, just checking."

It wasn't until Brianne got to the motel that evening she had a chance to relax. Beth had been busy playing all day and hadn't taken her regular nap, so she fell asleep fast. Once they had her in bed, her dad wanted to hear more about Jenna and Justine from her directly, and she told him. Her parents had agreed it would be best to wait until Jenna and Justine went home on Wednesday night and then for her mom to call Aunt Julie sometime after that.

They were also planning to drive down to Seattle tomorrow to spend Christmas Eve with her dad's family and come back late tomorrow night, so she wouldn't be seeing Jenna and Justine until Christmas Day. The next few days were kind of a blur for Brianne. She tried to enjoy being with her grandparents, aunts, uncles, and cousins, but she was changing from being a little girl into a teenager, and it seemed like a lot of them treated her differently. More than once she was asked if she had a boyfriend, and she got some interesting gifts, including sweatpants with the word "Princess" on the bottom from Aunt Julie and another pair in a different color from one of her cousins on her dad's side who had drawn her name this year.

She also got other clothes that weren't her style and a stationery set with a bunch of "teen-talk" as a background, and some of the phrases weren't good. She knew the giver probably didn't know what they meant, and she put it in with her other gifts but planned to throw it away when she got home.

It wasn't until Friday her mom and dad talked to her grandparents about Jenna and Justine, and they agreed Aunt Julie and Uncle Phil needed to know what Brianne had heard. While her mom made the call in the late afternoon, Brianne asked her dad for his phone again and she called Sarah, telling her about her interesting week.

Sarah agreed she had done the right thing, and then Sarah talked about her own week. She and Ryan had spent a lot of time together, and she had spent part of Christmas Eve with his family. He had given her a pretty necklace along with a Christian music CD, and Brianne suddenly remembered about the concert Austin had invited her to.

"He wrote to me this week and told me about it," Sarah said. "And I think we'll probably be able to meet you there."

Brianne asked the question on her mind. She had planned to write Sarah a letter this week, but she hadn't gotten around to it yet.

"What do you think he's doing, Sarah?"

"What do you mean?"

She didn't respond. She didn't know how to phrase it.

"I heard you went to the movies with him."

"He told you that?"

"No. Your mom did. I called on Saturday when you were gone."

Brianne had forgotten that. Her mom told her when she got home, and she had tried to call Sarah that evening, but she hadn't gotten a live response and hadn't left a message either.

"Do you think it's anything, or that he's just being a friend like he says?"

"What has he said exactly?"

She told her the comments he'd made about her dad, and the way Austin acted the night of the play. Speaking the words out loud, she knew what the answer was before Sarah said it.

"I think he likes you, but I also think he's willing to wait for the right time. Maybe that's why God moved me away, so Austin could see the light!"

They both laughed, and then Brianne groaned and laid on the bed. "I don't know if I'm ready for that."

"You don't have to do anything except be yourself and be friends for now. You can't go wrong doing that. Don't worry about the future, Bree. God will help you deal with it when it comes."

Chapter Three

When Brianne got off the phone with Sarah, she went downstairs and her dad said her mom was still talking to her aunt on the phone in the den. Going into the living room, she saw her grandmother there, and she went to sit beside her.

"You did the right thing, honey," she said, giving her hand a squeeze. "No matter how all of this turns out, don't question that, all right?"

"All right. What are you working on?"

Her grandma continued to knit the red yarn quickly and gracefully. "It's a scarf for the orphanage in Romania we send things to. Knitting is good for the soul at times like this."

"It's beautiful," she said, fingering the complex pattern in her grandmother's lap she had already completed.

"Would you like me to make you one while you're here? There's a bunch of yarn in that chest over there. You could pick what color you want."

"Sure," she said. Getting up from the couch to open the chest in the corner of the room, she began digging through the large assortment and found a multicolored pattern of pink, lavender, and white. She chose that one and took it back to where Grandma Anne was sitting.

"I can make it like this, or you can choose a different pattern," she said, handing her a knitting book called, *101 Knitting Projects.* "If you turn to the back, there are quite a few pages of different patterns to see. Pick whatever you like."

Brianne began scanning the colorful pictures of knitted yarn. Some of them were very complex and others were simpler. "Could you teach me how to knit?" she asked.

"Sure, if you'd like me to."

Once Brianne had selected a pattern she wanted, her grandmother took the book from her and put a check-mark beside her choice and a bookmark in the page, and then she set aside her current project and took out different knitting needles and a mostly used skein of yarn from her basket to show her how to cast on and make a row of basic stitches. She was about to have her try when her mom came into the room and their attention shifted to her.

"How did it go?" her grandmother asked, sounding concerned but not overly worried. She knew her daughters had good relationships with each other, and Grandma had been the one to tell her mom she thought the news would be best coming from her.

"Okay," her mom said. "She was really shocked about Jenna having a boyfriend. She had no idea. But she has suspected the thing about Justine. She's noticed she hasn't been eating well lately and seems concerned about her weight, but she didn't have any evidence to confront her about it."

"What is she going to do?"

"Talk to Phil first, and then they'll probably talk to Jenna and see how much she will admit to and then go from there. She thinks they'll have to get outside help for Justine, and I agree."

Brianne felt relieved her aunt believed her. One of her fears had been that Aunt Julie would think she was lying and then be mad at her and maybe her mom too.

"I told her we're going to be in Seattle again on Monday, so I might try and meet her for lunch somewhere," her mom went on. "She said there are other things she does know about she's not sure how to deal with. She said the same thing you did, honey, about them changing so fast she feels like she doesn't even know them right now."

"So Aunt Julie's not mad at me?"

"No, of course not. She's really glad you told me. It's hard, but she would rather know than have them doing stuff behind her back. She can't help them that way."

Brianne felt relieved, but she also felt concerned for her cousins. Just because their parents knew about it didn't mean they would be able to stop them from making dangerous choices.

Her dad came into the room. He'd heard her mom's voice and had come to hear the report, but his cell phone rang before her mom could say anything. Her dad used his phone mainly for church-related matters and had it with him in case there was some kind of problem that needed his immediate attention. Because he was on vacation, people wouldn't bother him otherwise, and it hadn't rung all week. Brianne could see that look in his eyes that said, 'I hope this isn't anything too serious.' Last summer when they had been here for two weeks, he'd gotten a call from Pastor Doug at the end of the first week telling him one of their long-term older members of the church had died, and the family wanted him to do the funeral, so he'd had to miss most of the second week of their vacation.

Her dad answered the call and had a serious expression on his face for a moment, but then he looked directly at her and smiled. "Oh, did she?" he said.

Brianne had no idea why he was looking at her like that until her dad said something else to the caller.

"I knew she tried to call Sarah, but I didn't know she called you too."

Brianne knew it was Austin, and she felt her heart start pounding really hard. Partly because he was calling her, but mostly because she hadn't said anything to her dad about calling Austin instead of Sarah when Sarah hadn't been home on Monday.

"Oh, I see," he said. "Well, here she is. Good talking to you, Austin. Say hello to your dad for me."

He held out the phone to her, and she felt super-embarrassed. *Austin! What are you doing calling me on my dad's cell phone? Are you crazy?*

"It's for you, sweetheart," he said. "Someone named Austin."

She took the phone from him and laughed nervously, responding to her dad's curious expression. "At least it's not work."

He smiled and she knew he wasn't mad, but she was going to have to explain herself. She said 'hello' to Austin, and wanted to be upset with him, but his words kept her from feeling that way.

"Hey. Sorry to bother you, but I was just thinking about you and wondering how everything turned out. Are you okay?"

"Yeah. I feel better now."

"You didn't tell your dad you called me?"

"No."

"Oops, sorry."

"That's okay. I'm glad you called. How are you?"

"Bored," he said.

She laughed and wandered into the hallway. He told her about his week, things he'd gotten for Christmas, and his plans to go snowboarding with Jason tomorrow and then with Michael's family for two days next week, but for now he didn't have much to do.

She told him a few more details about her cousins and what she had gotten for Christmas up here. "I got hot pink sweatpants that say Princess on them," she teased him.

"On the back?"

She laughed. "Yes."

"Please tell me you're not going to wear them."

"I'm not. My aunt left the tags on, so I'll be taking them back along with other things and getting something else. I'm like, 'Hello, just because I'm almost thirteen doesn't mean I want to start dressing like Fashion Barbie.'"

He laughed. "I'm glad, Brianne. I like the way you dress."

"You even like the pink?"

"Even the pink," he said. "It works for you."

"Thanks. And I like the way you dress. It's casual and comfortable but not like you have no idea what size you're supposed to wear."

"Like Michael, you mean?"

"Yes. You should give him advice about what girls are really looking for."

"And what are they looking for, besides the way they dress?"

"Someone who knows how to have a conversation and actually looks up when we're talking."

"Aww, he's just shy around you."

"What?"

"He has a major crush on you."

"Michael?"

He laughed. "Yes. Don't tell him I told you. He'd kill me."

Brianne wasn't at all excited about the prospect of Michael liking her. "I don't think I'll be letting him know I know that. I don't think I even want to know that."

"He's a good guy. I'm gonna' get him into church one of these days. I'm already talking to him about going to camp with us."

"Are you? That's great."

"I've gotten a definite 'maybe', so we'll see."

There was a pause in the conversation, and she knew she probably shouldn't talk too long, but she had been feeling lonely and bored today too, and talking to him was nice, even if she was going to have to explain herself to her dad once she hung up.

"I got my schedule for next semester in the mail today," he said.

"Did you?"

"Yep. I have all the same classes at the same times as before."

"I hope I do too then," she said. "Maybe I'll call Silas and ask him to open mine for me since they're getting our mail while we're gone."

"Calling *two* boys on your dad's phone while you're there? I don't know if you can get away with that."

"I can't believe you told him I called you."

"I thought he knew. Why didn't you tell him?"

"I asked him for it so I could call Sarah, but when I couldn't reach her, I called you instead, and then when I gave it back to him, I just didn't tell him. I don't know why."

"He knows we're just friends, right?"

"Yes."

"I should let you go then so he doesn't get the wrong idea."

She laughed. "That would probably be good."

"Okay, see you next Sunday. I hope your second week is better than the first."

"Me too. Thanks for calling. I really do appreciate your friendship, Austin. Even if you do get me in trouble here."

"I don't think your mom and dad are too worried about you, Brianne. You're the most responsible, honest, and caring seventh grade girl I know."

"Yeah, well, pray for me," she laughed. "See you next week."

She lowered the phone from her ear and clicked it off. Going back into the living room, deciding she may as well get this over with, she handed the phone back to her dad. Her grandmother was talking, so he took it from her and didn't say anything. But he pulled her toward him, and she sat on his lap, not quite fitting there the way she used to, but it gave her that same loved and safe feeling it always had.

Her grandmother set her knitting aside when she finished talking about the latest new developments at their church. Her grandma was a diehard prayer warrior and had been praying for revival in their small church for quite some time, and it sounded like things were going better now than they had for a few years.

"I should get started on something for us to eat for dinner," she said, getting up from the couch and heading for the kitchen. Her mom went to help her, and once it was just her and her dad in the room, he asked the question she was expecting.

"Why didn't you tell me you had called Austin?"

"I tried to call Sarah, but she wasn't home and wasn't answering her phone, so I called Austin instead. I just didn't mention it."

"Are you still just friends?"

"Yes."

"Are you sure Austin knows that?"

"Yes. And if that ever changes—not that I think it's going to anytime soon, but if it does, I promise not to keep it from you."

"I know you wouldn't," he said. "You have too honest of a heart for that."

"Where's Beth?" she asked, suddenly realizing she hadn't come into the room with him. She had been clinging to either herself or her mom and dad all week.

"Playing *Pretty Pretty Princess* with Grandpa."

She laughed. "If she can talk you into it, then I know she didn't have any trouble getting Grandpa to play."

"He used to play with you too. Do you remember?"

She didn't think she did and knew it must have been when she was really little, but she did remember her dad playing it with her, and she told him so.

"Speaking of princesses," he said. "I know those pants were a gift—"

She stopped him before he finished his sentence. "I'm going to exchange them."

"Good."

"I'd rather have some that say "Super Cute.""

He started tickling her, and she screamed and fled from his lap as soon as she was able to break free. He didn't come after her, but her mom came into the room to see what was going on. Once she saw her on the floor, smiling and laughing at her dad, her mom walked over and put her hands on his shoulders.

"What are you doing?"

"Tickling our daughter, and she deserved it."

"Is this true, Brianne?"

"Yes," she said, lying on her back in the middle of the living room floor and smiling at her parents. "But it was worth it."

"Does this have anything to do with a certain youth pastor's son calling you on your dad's cell phone?"

"No," she laughed. "But I think I've reached Daddy's limit for today."

"For the year," he said.

She smiled. "Lucky for me, a new one starts in five days."

Chapter Four

Brianne's second week of Winter Break was much more uneventful than the first. They went to her grandparents' church on Sunday, and she thought it was nice to sit with her whole family instead of having her mom helping with the children and her dad being up front most of the time.

On Monday they went to Seattle to see Grandma and Grandpa Carmichael again, and they went on a ferry boat ride around Puget Sound in the afternoon, which she enjoyed but Steven absolutely loved. He liked anything having to do with water, and Brianne stayed with him much of the time since he wanted to be out on the deck of the boat rather than inside where it was warmer. But she didn't mind. She liked the feel of the wind on her face and watching the boat make its way through the water.

On New Year's Eve they were back in Bellingham, and her grandparents' church had a thing that went until midnight where there was lots of food and activities going on for people of every age. Brianne spent much of the time with Beth in the children's room where they were playing games and then watched a movie. Many of them ended up falling asleep before midnight, including Beth.   There were adults supervising the room, and she could have left Beth lying there, but she didn't want her sister to wake up and be surrounded by strangers, so she stayed.

Her dad came to find her around ten-thirty, and he took her place so she could go have fun.   The youth group, which was similar in size to hers, was having a bonfire in a vacant field behind the church.   They were roasting hot dogs and marshmallows and just having fun.   She went to join them, and everyone was friendly and welcoming.   She had met some of them before when she had visited her grandparents in the past. There was one particular girl who reminded her of Sarah, and they always got along well.   She was glad to see that even though Katie was in seventh grade like herself, she hadn't changed much—at least not any more than she had, and they still had a lot in common.

When it was getting close to midnight, two boys came over to talk to Katie, and they sat with them as they sang songs and the youth leader gave a brief devotional about setting goals for themselves in the new year concerning their relationship with God.

One of the boys, whose name was Alex, obviously liked Katie.   Brianne didn't know if Katie could see it. Brianne remembered Alex and knew they had grown up going to church together, so Katie likely saw him as a friend—or at least figured that's the way he saw her.

The other one was a friend of Alex's that Brianne hadn't met before, so she didn't know if he had moved here recently or if Alex knew him from school and had invited him to come.   His name was Derek, and he was nice like Alex, only quieter. And she wasn't sure what it was about him, but he reminded her of Joel.

She had spent a lot of New Year's Eves with the West family at the camp. A few times it had been cold enough for them to go ice sliding on the lake, and there had often been snow on the ground. Joel would get out a bag of fireworks he'd saved from the Fourth of July and they would go into the field and set them off, watching the beautiful colors light up the night and reflect off the blanket of snow crystals on the ground.

Sitting there as those around her were counting down the final seconds to midnight, she suddenly felt lonely for him. She missed all of her friends, but many of them she would be seeing in a few days. But she probably wouldn't be seeing Joel until this summer, and right now that seemed like a long time to wait.

Saying good night to Katie and the others when it was time to leave, Brianne didn't expect to be seeing any of them until her family returned for another visit, but Katie asked if she was busy on Friday, saying they were all going bowling and to play laser-tag, and she invited her to come. Brianne said she would ask and thanked her for the invitation.

Her mom and dad said it was fine if she wanted to go, and other than learning how to knit from her grandmother and making significant progress on a simple scarf, going with the youth group on Friday was the only eventful part of her week. They drove back home on Saturday. Silas had seen they were home, and he walked up to bring their mail at seven-thirty.

He said he couldn't stay long, but she gave him a brief run-down of her vacation.

Her dad sorted through the mail, and she had two letters waiting for her from Sarah and also one from Joel. She also had received her new class schedule, and she opened it, smiling when she saw it had remained the same. She almost called Austin to tell him but decided to wait until she saw him at church in the morning.

In one of Sarah's letters she told her Ryan had asked for permission to kiss her at midnight on New Year's Eve, and she had been tempted to let him, but she had told him no. He was fine with waiting, but he couldn't help letting her know he wanted to. Brianne was proud of her and wrote a letter telling her so.

She waited until later to open Joel's letter. It was partly because she was interrupted while responding to Sarah's, and she wanted to wait until she wouldn't be interrupted before reading his. After Beth was asleep and Brianne had brushed her teeth and gotten into her pajamas, she took the letter from the envelope. Reading the first line, she remembered she had sent him the Christmas gift before they left, and he was thanking her for that and said he would be having pictures taken for her with the disposable camera she'd sent him.

Since she was asking for pictures of him, she had included two pictures of herself in the Christmas card she sent with his gift. One was her school picture from this year, and the other one had been a snapshot her mom had taken when she had been outside this fall raking leaves in the front yard, that she thought was particularly good. Sometimes indoor pictures of her didn't turn out well because she had very light skin, and the flash tended to make her look washed-out, but outdoor pictures in the natural light came out much better.

Thanks for the pictures too. I think you are very pretty, Brianne. I was comparing this year's picture with the one from fifth grade that you gave me right before you moved, and you've changed a lot—but in good ways. Don't try to change anything. You're perfect just the way you are.

I was looking at the camp schedule for this summer, and there are two weeks that look good for me. One is the last week in July and the other is the final week of camp in August, so if either of those work for you, let me know and I'll sign up for the same one.

Joel

At this point she didn't know which week would be better. In the past her family had gone to Washington sometime in late June, and last summer she had gone up by herself on the train in July, but that was flexible. She would have to talk to Sarah and Austin and find out when would be a good time for them.

Finishing up her letter to Sarah before going to sleep, she mentioned those two weeks and also asked if she might want to go with her to visit her grandparents this summer. She thought that would be a lot of fun to travel with her and have someone her age to hang out with while she was there.

***

On Sunday morning Pastor Doug had an announcement to make that she found exciting. He usually played guitar and Austin played drums during their singing time, but he wanted to try to put together a more complete band. He invited anyone who wanted to be a part of it to sign up if they wanted to play an instrument or be one of the vocalists.

Emily was sitting next to her, and she signed up to play keyboard, and she saw that Danielle had an interest in being one of the singers. Brianne decided to write she could either sing or play flute. Pastor Doug passed the list around again on Thursday night at youth group and announced they would be having their first rehearsal on Saturday at six o'clock, one hour before a scheduled youth activity where they would be gathering at Austin's house for pizza and a movie.

On Friday morning Austin had some news to share with her. One of the areas that would be lacking in the band was an electric guitar player. Austin was learning, but he wasn't very good yet, and he needed to play drums anyway, but apparently Michael had been taking lessons for two years and was quite good.

"When I mentioned that to my dad, he said I should ask him if he wants to play with us, so I called him last night, and he said he would be willing to give it a try."

"That's great," she said. Remembering Austin's effort to get Michael to go to camp this summer, she mentioned the two weeks that were good for Joel, and he said he would talk to his mom and dad and to Michael and see if one week would be better than another. She had already gotten a letter back from Sarah that said either week was fine for her and she would love to go with her to Washington sometime.

Saturday's rehearsal was a lot of fun. Pastor Doug wanted her to sing on some songs and play her flute for the slower ones he thought it would sound nice for, and there was only one song she thought was too hard because it was in a weird key she wasn't used to playing in.

Michael was there too, and he did play electric guitar well. Brianne had been feeling a little strange around him since Austin had told her he liked her, but at the same time she didn't really feel that way about him, so she tried to be her normal self. He went to Austin's house for pizza and a movie with everyone too, and he seemed to have a good time.

Another addition to the group that evening was Marissa's brother Miguel and his girlfriend. Marissa had been trying to get Miguel to come to youth group or an activity for the last couple of months, and she had finally succeeded. Brianne noticed Danielle making an effort to get to know him and Andrea. They were the same age and knew each other from school.

When she got home, Brianne made a point of telling her dad there had been a good turnout tonight, including those who attended regularly and the newcomers. She knew he had been praying for better attendance, and he commented on how Pastor Doug's idea for the youth band had been a good one, and they both hoped it would spark some life into the group that had been slowly losing momentum ever since they had started the new building project last year. If all went well, the new building would be completed sometime this summer, and they were hoping to have enough kids to make good use of it.

The following afternoon Brianne was outside petting her cats on the front porch when her dad came home from a meeting he'd had after church. He smiled at her and gave her a kiss on the forehead, but she could tell he looked bothered by something. She wasn't sure who he'd had a meeting with, and after a minute she went inside to see if she could find out what was going on. Often her dad would talk to her mom when he came home from a difficult meeting, and upon entering the house, she could see them standing in the kitchen.

Walking quietly to the wall that separated the kitchen from the dining room area, she stayed out of sight and listened. The only reason she felt especially concerned was because she knew lately there had been some people in the church who had been criticizing new ideas and changes her dad had been making, and she had two main fears. One was that her dad would be asked to leave the church if there were enough people who didn't agree with what he was doing, and the second was that her dad would choose to leave if he felt there was too much opposition to his leadership.

Either one would mean the same thing: They would have to move, and she would have to start all over again. A new school. A new church. And new friends.

Chapter Five

"So, they liked the idea?" Brianne heard her mom say.

"Yeah, they did," her dad replied. "They think it would be a good move."

"Then why do you look like they said no?"

"When I called Doug to tell him, he said he's not sure he's the right man for the job."

"What? Why would he say that?"

"He thinks if we're going to start paying someone to run the youth program full-time, then we should hire someone younger who actually has a degree in youth ministry."

"He'd be willing to give up his job?"

"Yep. And not just willing, but he thinks we should definitely go that route. He told me if we offer him the job, he won't take it."

Her mom laughed. "You never thought Doug would be the one you would have to fight on this, did you?"

"No."

"Do you think he's right?"

"I don't know. Maybe. But I'd hate to see that happen. He's the one who's gotten the program to where it is today. He had the vision for the new building, and he has a heart for these kids. We've had a slump lately, but I'm not sure that's his fault. Just a different set of kids than he's had before."

"Well, you yourself said it doesn't have to happen right away. Maybe if you give him time to think about it, he will hear God telling him otherwise and decide to stay."

"And if he doesn't? Should I go ahead and propose we hire someone full-time, or keep things as they are?"

"Maybe you should give God time to speak to you about that."

The talking ceased, and Brianne knew her mother had given Daddy that look that made him kiss her and silently agree to give this decision more thought and prayer. Brianne hadn't known her dad had been thinking of trying to get Pastor Doug a full-time position as their youth pastor instead of only being part-time. He worked as a building contractor the rest of the time to support his family.

As far as Brianne was concerned, she thought he would do a great job, but the possibility of losing him as her youth pastor wasn't her primary concern. Did this mean Austin's family might move? Maybe he didn't want to be a full-time youth pastor, but maybe he would still want to work part-time at another small church that could only afford to hire someone like him. As a building contractor, she knew he could do that anywhere. And the thought of Austin moving away made her want to scream.

No! Not Austin too. God, you can't do that!

She wanted to march into the kitchen and tell her dad he couldn't let that happen, but she wasn't supposed to be eavesdropping, and she didn't know if it would make any difference anyway. It wasn't her dad she had to convince. It was Pastor Doug. But how could she do that without giving away that she knew?

Slowly stepping away, she went to her room and finished up her homework. She tried to tell herself she was worried about nothing. That either Pastor Doug would end up taking the job, or that he wouldn't, but the Lockharts wouldn't move. But she didn't know for certain, and her fear that her own family would end up moving again in another year or sooner crept back in, and she wished she could make time freeze. Other than Sarah living away from here, her life was really good right now. She was enjoying school, had good friends, was involved in activities she enjoyed—just like before they had moved the last time.

She wanted to say something to Austin about it the following day, but she didn't know if he would know about it. There were times she didn't know about decisions her parents were considering until after they had already made them.

She didn't hear her dad, Pastor Doug, or anyone in the church say anything about it for the next several weeks, but it came to mind often. One Sunday the lesson in class was on not worrying about what the future held and living one day at a time, and she tried to do that, but it wasn't easy.

She said something to Joel about it in a letter she wrote to him in late January. She needed to express her fears to someone, and he was the only person she was close to who didn't know Austin and his family.

***

As Brianne's thirteenth birthday drew near, Austin kept her informed of the specific plans he was making for them. His dad was going to be driving them into Portland on the night of the concert, and Sarah and Ryan would be meeting them there along with two of Sarah's other friends. Sarah's brother, Scott, would be driving them, and he was going to meet Pastor Doug there and go someplace close by to hang out and talk. Before they had moved away, Scott had been a strong member of the youth group, and Pastor Doug had been his youth pastor for five years, so Austin said his dad was looking forward to getting together with him and finding out how he was doing.

Brianne debated about asking any of her other friends to go, even though Austin had said she could. She felt like Austin wanted to make it special for her, and she didn't want to turn it into a big group thing, but she didn't want to invite two or three friends and leave everyone else out. In the end she let it be known they were going but didn't specifically invite anyone to come along, and the only ones who said anything about wanting to go too were Silas and Danielle, which was fine with her. They got their own tickets and would be riding with them.

The other thing she debated about was spending that weekend with Sarah rather than coming back home on Friday night after the concert. Sarah invited her to stay until Monday because it was President's Day, and she wanted to, but at the same time she knew her family would want to celebrate her birthday, and she didn't want to do it early or wait until sometime the following week, so she decided to try and visit Sarah another time.

Both her birthday and the concert were on Friday, and it was also Valentine's Day which had always been kind of fun. She expected to get birthday presents from her family and Sarah, but since she wasn't having a party, she didn't really expect to get any from anyone else. But when she came home from school she had a package waiting for her from Joel. Along with a wrapped present, he had also returned the camera she'd sent him for Christmas and a letter responding to the one she had sent him.

Hi, Brianne. Happy Birthday! That's from everyone in my family, not just me, and so is the gift. We hope you like it.

Have you heard any more about your youth pastor and his family possibly moving? If they are, I'm sorry. I know that would be hard. But if you don't know any more than when you wrote to me, I thought I'd share something with you I didn't realize until I read your letter.

I've spent the last two years keeping myself sort of closed off from new people. The friends I had when you were here are still my friends, but I haven't really made any new ones, and those I already know I haven't made as much of a part of my life as you were when you were here.

You moving away was really hard for me. I know I didn't really say so, but I felt alone for a long time after you were gone. I had other friends, but not like you. Not someone I always had fun with and could be completely just me.

I'm going to give you some advice, and I know I need to follow it myself. We can't live always wondering, 'What if I get really close to that person and then one of us moves away?' I know with your dad being a pastor, the possibility is high you will move again before you graduate from high school, and maybe more than once. I have that here too. Right now my dad is running this camp, but it's not a lifetime thing. By this time next year we could be living at another camp who-knows-where, or my dad could be doing something completely different.

But I think we have to just live today and let God take care of where we go next, who we leave behind, or who leaves us behind, you know? Don't stop your friendship with Austin or even hold back just because he might not be there next month. Live for today. Don't cheat yourself or any of your friends out of special times because you're scared. I've been doing that, and I know I need to stop. Pray for me in this and I'll pray for you too, okay?

I hope you have fun at the concert. It's not a date, huh? Are you sure he knows that?

Joel

She knew Joel was right, and she also knew she had been doing that exact thing. Ever since she'd heard about Pastor Doug possibly stepping down as their youth pastor, she had been holding Austin at a bit of a distance. He had asked her to do some things with her outside of school and church a few times, and she had made up excuses why she couldn't and kept their phone conversations short when he had called her.

He was still in all of her classes, and she saw him at church on Sundays, Thursdays, and often on Saturdays too, so she was never away from him for long, but emotionally she had withdrawn a little bit from where they had been at Christmas. She had been looking forward to tonight and dreading it at the same time. She loved spending time with Austin. It was always fun and easy. Just like it had always been with Sarah and with Joel.

Austin and his dad came to pick her up at five, and after stopping to pick up Silas and Danielle, they were on their way. Silas and Danielle had a gift for her along with Austin, and she opened them in the van as they were driving. Silas and his sister were in the middle seat of the van, and she and Austin were in the back.

Silas and Danielle had gotten her a gift card to the Christian bookstore in Longview, and she thanked them sincerely for the generous amount. And then she opened Austin's gift, saying that taking her to the concert tonight was more than enough of a gift, but he reminded her that the concert had been her Christmas present, not for her birthday.

Opening the box, she found two things inside, and she gave him a look that said one would have been enough. "You got me two gifts?" she said, picking up the CD she didn't have yet and had planned to buy at the concert tonight, but now she wouldn't have to.

"The other one is for Valentine's Day," he whispered in her ear.

She took the smaller white box and removed the pink ribbon surrounding it. Opening the lid, she gasped at what she saw. It was a beautiful silver necklace with her name spelled in a loopy script and a pink diamond-like stone in the top loop of the B.

"Where did you find this?" she asked. She rarely found things with her name, let alone something that also had her favorite color to make it absolutely perfect.

"I had it made," he said. "Just for you. There's not another one like it."

"Austin!"

He smiled and took it out of the box to help her put it on. Danielle and Silas turned around to see what she had gotten, and she modeled it for them once Austin had secured the clasp at the back of her neck.

"That's really pretty," Danielle said. "Did you pick that out, Austin?"

"I ordered it off the Internet," he said like it was no big deal. "Just someplace that makes custom-designed stuff."

Brianne exchanged a look with Danielle only girls would understand. She felt grateful when Danielle didn't say anything but turned around and let her express her own feelings on the matter. Once Silas had turned around also, she looked at Austin and didn't hold back like she might have done before she had received Joel's letter. She told him exactly what she was thinking.

"Thank you. I love it," she said, fingering the delicate metal that fell just below her collar bone.

"You're welcome," he said. "I'm glad you like it."

She smiled and leaned over to give him a kiss on the cheek. "I don't like it, Austin. I love it."

Chapter Six

Arriving in Portland at six-fifteen, Pastor Doug found a place to park the van near the concert hall, and they walked to a nearby restaurant to get dinner. They were going to be meeting Sarah and the others at seven, and the concert was scheduled to begin at seven-thirty. They had reserved seats near the front on the main floor, so there was no reason to try and get there early.

They were seated in a circular corner booth, and Brianne sat in the middle with Austin on one side of her and Danielle on the other. Over the last two months, she had been getting to know Silas' sister pretty well, and even though she was almost sixteen, Danielle didn't act like she was above going to a concert with a bunch of seventh graders.

Brianne ordered a grilled-cheese sandwich, and Austin laughed at her. "It's your birthday. You can get something better than that."

"I like grilled-cheese sandwiches," she said. "And I'm not that hungry anyway. I ate something before we left."

Brianne didn't know if Austin noticed her mood shift from the way she had been around him the last

53

several weeks, but as the evening progressed, he began teasing her more and more, and Brianne knew Joel had been right about not letting her fears about the future take away from her current joy.

Because she hadn't seen Sarah since before Christmas, long before she had become more cautious around Austin, she was surprised when Sarah said something to her about it in the bathroom during intermission.

"You and Austin are really getting close, aren't you?"

"What makes you say that?"

"You never used to act that way around him."

"What way?"

"Like you are tonight. I sort of noticed it when I came to the play, but now it's really obvious."

"What's obvious?"

"He's your best friend."

"You're still my best friend, Sarah."

"I don't mean like he's your best friend, so I'm not. I mean like you have two now. Me and him. But you're friends with him in a different way than you are with me."

Brianne didn't comment further. She knew that was true. When she had first seen Sarah tonight, she had begun to regret her decision to not stay with her this weekend, knowing their time together would be so short. But after spending the last hour with Austin on one side of her and Sarah on the other, she knew she enjoyed their company equally. If she was going back tonight without being as close to Austin as she was, it would be harder. But his friendship would help her to be all right with having to leave Sarah behind.

When they returned to their seats, Brianne was reminded the whole reason she was here tonight was because of Austin. He had brought her to see two of her favorite Christian groups perform. He had gotten great seats. And he'd arranged for her to have time with her other best friend she didn't get to see much.

Before the second band came out on stage, she turned to him while Sarah was busy talking to Ryan, and she made a special point to thank him. "This has been so fun," she said, feeling like she might cry. "Thanks for making my birthday so special. I've never had anybody do something like this for me."

He smiled, and Brianne had no idea what he was thinking. Boys were so hard to read. They could be obvious if they wanted to be. When Austin had liked Sarah, he'd been pretty bold about letting her know that. But with her, he was mostly just himself, and she didn't know if it was because he didn't have any feelings for her beyond friendship whatsoever, or if he just wasn't saying it. But his actions to bring all of this together told her he cared about her and he liked spending time with her.

She didn't say anything else, and the lights went down almost immediately after she spoke. The music began, and the all-girl group came out on stage. Brianne enjoyed every second of listening to the familiar songs and some new ones. But the most special part of all of this was being here with Austin. Even more than Sarah.

Before they sang one of her favorite songs, they talked about going through hard times and trusting God, and also leaning on your friends and allowing them to be there for you. One thing Brianne had been wondering about was how she could ever repay Austin for tonight. What special thing could she do for him? But she didn't have any solid ideas and knew there was likely no way she could top this, so she decided maybe she should just let it be. To let Austin treat her special without having to do anything in return.

After the concert when she had to say good-bye to Sarah, it was hard, but not as difficult as when she'd come to her play. Hugging her good-bye made her cry, but her tears weren't so much about Sarah. They were about Austin and what she would do if he was suddenly out of her life too.

Walking back to the van, she decided to say something she knew she could say without giving away she knew anything about the possibility of him moving. If Austin knew anything about it, his response might give that away, but it wasn't why she said it. She said it because it was the truth.

"You better not move away too."

He laughed. "Us leave Clatskanie? Yeah right. You, on the other hand, I worry about that."

"About what?"

"Your family moving."

"You do?"

"Sure. You know what the longest amount of time is that any pastor has been at this church since I was born?"

"How long?"

"Four years. Your dad's already been here two."

"Yeah, I know. And we were only in Sweet Home for six, and my dad loved that church."

"What are you saying? He doesn't love us?"

"No," she laughed. "But some people give him a hard time."

"I know. My dad too. But he's a lifer, so he doesn't care."

"A lifer?"

"He grew up in this church. My grandfather helped start it. He'll be here until he dies."

"Even if he's not the youth pastor anymore?"

"Yeah, in fact he might not be for much longer."

"You know about that?"

"Sure. Do you?"

"I don't think I'm supposed to, but I overheard my mom and dad talking. How do you feel about it?"

"About them hiring another youth pastor?"

"Yes."

They were getting close to the van, and everyone was ahead of them, so they stopped walking to finish this conversation. "I'd be fine with it. I think it's cool your dad actually talked the Board into hiring someone full-time. My dad too. I think he just wants to get out of the way and let your dad get things going that are long overdue."

"And you wouldn't move?"

"No. Is that what you thought?"

She nodded.

He looked at her like her recent distant behavior suddenly made sense. "My dad took the job because no one else would. I mean, he likes it, but he's been praying for a long time for someone else. He's a builder, not a pastor."

Neither of them said anything else until they were in the van and on their way home. Brianne felt relieved Austin's family had no plans to move, but the fear remained that she would be the one moving soon.

She was deep in thought, remembering how hard leaving her friends behind in Sweet Home had been, and how leaving Clatskanie at this time in her life would be even more difficult.

"It's still you're birthday," Austin whispered in her ear. "You can't be sad on your birthday. It's not allowed."

She looked at him and smiled. "We're not moving today, right?"

"And I'm sure you won't for awhile. I shouldn't have said that about no one being here longer than four years. Your dad will probably be here for twenty."

"That would be nice," she said.

"Not that you need to worry. You can make friends anywhere, Brianne. You moved here and met Sarah on the first day. She moved and now you have more friends than when she was here."

"But I miss her, and Joel."

"Would you miss me?"

"Of course I would. I missed you when we were in Washington for two weeks."

"You did?"

"Yes," she laughed and then whispered. "And you didn't miss me? Mr. 'Call me on my dad's cell phone'?"

"Did you get in trouble for that?"

"No."

"Have you heard anything more about your cousins since you've been back?"

"A little from my mom. She's talked to my aunt several times, and they're having a hard time with Jenna, but Justine has been seeing a counselor and is okay now. Apparently she hadn't been doing it for very long, so it was easy for her to stop."

"Jenna's the one with the boyfriend?"

"Yes. She's not supposed to be seeing him anymore, but it's not like they can know where she is every minute."

Brianne felt tired, and she turned sideways so she could lay her head against the seat. There was a time not that long ago when she could curl up in the back seat of their van that was similar to the Lockhart's and fall asleep. But it wasn't as comfortable now. Her legs were too long, and her head went too far above the backrest.

"Come here," Austin said. "You can use my shoulder for a pillow."

She turned back so her body was facing the front, and she leaned her head against Austin's shoulder. She had to scrunch down in the seat a little, but it worked.

"I can't believe how tall you're getting," she said. "Six months ago we were the same height."

"Like Sarah and Ryan, you mean?"

"Yes."

"Those two are too perfect for each other," Austin said.

"Do you like him?"

"Sure. He seems nice."

"Was it hard for you to see them together?"

"No. Not really. If Sarah's happy, that's good enough for me."

"You're so sweet. Do you know how many guys wouldn't give a second thought to Sarah's happiness? They would just be wishing they were holding her hand instead."

"If she still lived in Clatskanie, I'd probably feel that way, but she doesn't, so it's not that tough."

"So you're officially over her?"

"I guess so."

Brianne closed her eyes, feeling too tired to respond, even though it was huge. Austin had liked Sarah for a long time. She remembered it had been last Valentine's Day when he first told Sarah he liked her. He'd given her a Valentine card that was like a multiple choice quiz. The question was: On Valentine's Day I can_____. And the choices were: A) Kiss you; B) Marry you; C) Call you sweetheart; or D) Take a hike.

Sarah had made a fifth choice that said: E) Be my friend, and then she'd written him a nice note about how she didn't want to be more than friends with guys yet but she did think he was very sweet.

Brianne fingered the necklace Austin had given her, and she smiled. "Thanks again for the necklace," she said. "You never gave Sarah anything this nice."

"That's because Sarah was never my best friend."

"But you wanted her to be."

"No, I don't think that's what I wanted. I wanted Sarah to be my girlfriend."

She understood what he meant. "So, now that you're over her, who's taking her place? I know there has to be someone you have your eye on."

"Yeah, there's someone," he said.

"Who? No, wait. Let me see if I can guess." She gave him her three top choices, but he said no to every one.

"Okay, I give up. Who is she?"

"You," he said.

"Ha, ha. Very funny. Is there really someone, or are you—"

"I'm not joking, Brianne."

She lifted her head from his shoulder and looked at him. Lights from a car traveling behind them made his face easy to see. He appeared serious.

"You're not?"

"No."

She wasn't sure what to say. Had she somehow misled him into thinking she wanted them to be more than friends? She thought they had been honest with each other about that, but maybe she needed to remind him. Just to be clear.

"But we are just friends, right?"

"Yes."

"But you want to change that?"

"Not right now. I'd rather have you as a best friend than a girlfriend, but maybe someday you could be both."

Brianne felt her heart start pounding really hard. Austin didn't say stuff like that unless he meant it. She'd had occasional thoughts about having Austin as her boyfriend someday, but it had all been in her head. But this was reality. He was saying it.

"What would you do if I decided I want a boyfriend now?"

"Me, or someone else?"

"Either."

"I don't think you want that."

"Why?"

"Because you've told me you don't."

"I could change my mind."

"But that's not you."

She smiled. He was right. She'd had the opportunity with Silas, and now with Austin too, but she wasn't taking it. Even with Sarah having a boyfriend, she still didn't want that for herself yet. But she did want guys like Silas and Austin and Joel as friends, and she was glad she had them.

Laying her head back on his shoulder, she closed her eyes and knew this day was coming to a perfect end. She had loved going to the concert, being with her friends, and was thankful for all of the things she had gotten for her thirteenth birthday and Valentine's Day.

But the best gift of all was sitting right beside her.

Chapter Seven

When Brianne arrived home from school on the Wednesday following her birthday, she found the packet of pictures on her bed from the one-time use camera she had sent to Joel for Christmas. Her mom had taken it to be developed for her on Saturday and then picked them up today.

Opening the packet and flipping through the pictures, she saw Joel had done what she expected. There were some pictures of him but also several of his family, the lake, a nice sunset, and a view of the camp from the lookout tower.

There were two pictures of him she really liked. One was of him holding a fish he had caught at the river, and another was of him sitting on the ground in his front yard beside his dog, Sam. In his letter he had included his school photo from this year, and she had already placed it on her bulletin board above her headboard. She made room for the other two pictures of him, along with the shot from the lookout tower: a wide-angle view of the lake and surrounding area. The others she put away for now. She was in the process of putting together a scrapbook of her friends, having pages that were specific to each friend. She had finished the ones she'd made of Sarah, but she still had a lot of work to do on the others.

There was something else on her bed she picked up after returning from her desk. Her mom had gotten the mail today, and there was a letter from her cousin Justine. She didn't have any idea what to expect and prepared herself for it being a letter where Justine told her she felt betrayed because of what she had told her mom, but even if it was, she knew she had done the right thing. She wanted her cousins to still like her and hoped they could have fun times again together in the future, but she had prepared herself for that not being the case, especially if Jenna and Justine didn't change back to the way they once had been.

Dear Brianne,

Hi. How are you? I remembered today that your birthday was on Friday. I'm sorry I missed it. Christmas seems like a long time ago. I'm doing better now though, and I wanted to write and thank you for what you did. I was mad at first, but I'm not now. I may not be the size I want to be, but I feel so much better, and I'm learning to accept the way God has made me. I wish I was as thin as you and Jenna, but I'm not, and the doctor tells me I can't be that thin unless I make myself sick, and I really hated doing that.

I'd like to say Jenna is doing better, but she's not. In a way she got me started with not eating right. She has a couple of friends she's been hanging around that she tries to be like, and when she started sneaking out and stuff, I knew I could never do anything like that because I'm too much of a chicken, and her friends don't really like me anyway. I wanted to be thin like them, and I also wanted to do something that I knew wasn't right. I'm not sure why. Maybe because she was doing it and getting away with it, and once I started, I had this feeling of power like I could be bad like her. I know it sounds stupid, but that's how I felt at the time.

But now I'm more worried about her than anything. She's not listening to my mom and dad, or me. Just her friends. I don't know what to do and neither do my parents, so I guess we just have to pray. Could you pray for her too?

Anyway, I just wanted to say happy birthday, and I'm sorry you had such a bad Christmas because of us. I don't know about Jenna, but I'll look forward to seeing you sometime this summer.

Love,
Justine

Brianne wrote Justine back and told her she would be praying for Jenna. She also shared something with her that had happened yesterday. She'd been reading a book, one Sarah had given to her on Friday night, and there had been a scene between two friends where one of the girls had been trying to be good at basketball like her friend was, but she wasn't as good. She ended up getting mad at her over something else, but at the root of her anger was the feeling she wasn't good at anything like her friend.

Once her friend found out she was trying to be like her, she said, "You don't have to be anyone for me except yourself. I don't want you as my friend because you're like me. I want you as my friend because you're you. If I wanted someone like me, I'd go find her!"

When I read that I realized I do that sometimes with my friends too. I think I have to try and be like them or they won't like me, but real friends don't do that.

I also feel like I heard God speaking to me when I read the words, "You don't have to be anyone for me except yourself." Sometimes I feel like I fall so short of what God wants me to be, but He just wants me to be me. He tells me what kinds of choices I should be making, but not because He expects me to be perfect. He just wants the best for me and He knows what that is!

Brianne finished the letter by saying she would be happy to hear from her anytime, either by letter or over the phone. Her mom asked her about the letter when she went to get a snack, and Brianne told her most of what Justine had said. Brianne had thought of an idea, and she asked her mom about it.

"I was thinking of inviting Jenna and Justine to go to camp with me this summer. Do you think that would be okay?"

"Sure, honey. I think that's a great idea."

"Do you think they would be able to go?"

"I don't know. You could always ask. Have you decided when you're going?"

"I think the last week in August is going to be best for everybody here that wants to go, and Sarah too. Marissa's family is going on vacation in July, and so is Ryan's."

On Saturday Brianne got two more camp brochures from Pastor Doug and planned to send them to her cousins, telling them the week she was going. She wouldn't be surprised if Jenna didn't want to go, but she hoped Justine would even if her sister didn't.

Worship band rehearsal was fun like usual, and after practicing for the past six weeks, Pastor Doug thought they were ready to start playing for the group on Sunday mornings and Thursday nights. They went through all the songs they were planning to do tomorrow, and Brianne was playing her flute on two of them and singing along with Danielle on the others. Danielle had a really pretty voice and often harmonized while Brianne sang the melody.

Brianne knew she had a decent voice. She had been singing in church as far back as she could remember, and others had told her she sang well before. But Danielle's voice had something extra that made the song come alive somehow. She sang with such passion and a love for God, and Brianne really enjoyed singing with her. She told her so when they had finished and were waiting for her dad to come pick them up.

"Thanks," Danielle said. "I love singing."

"Have you ever been in a worship band like this before?"

"No. I was in a garage band when we lived in California, and I sang the lead vocals, but we weren't singing praise music. I'm glad Pastor Doug is giving me a chance to do this here."

Marissa and her brother Miguel came over to say good night as they headed for the door. Marissa had been with them from the beginning. She played flute in band at school, but for this she was playing guitar along with Pastor Doug. She had been taking lessons for about a year, but she wanted to learn how to play worship music, so he was teaching her.

Pastor Doug had learned her brother knew how to play bass guitar. There was another high school guy who did too, but he could only come on Sundays, so Pastor Doug had asked Miguel if he could practice with them and begin playing on Thursday nights. Miguel had been coming every week since.

Danielle told her privately that Miguel and his girlfriend, Andrea, were on her "lost sheep" list— people she prayed for regularly and did everything she could to let them know she cared about them, and then she would patiently wait for when she had an opportunity to talk to them about God and why they needed Him. It was obvious just by the way Miguel interacted with Danielle she had done a good job of being a friend and making him feel welcome here.

Danielle had made an incredible turnaround in the last three months, and Brianne had a hard time putting her finger on why at first. But watching and listening to her sing tonight, she had figured it out. Brianne had memorized the verse, *"Delight yourself in the LORD and he will give you the desires of your heart."* And she had been trying to enjoy her relationship with God more than she ever had before, but the progress had been slow.

She got caught up in thinking it was about being good and right, instead of being loved and forgiven. So when she had bad days and didn't feel like she had been a very good friend or sister, or she got busy with school and didn't have time to read her Bible, she would start feeling guilty and disgusted with herself.

But then this Voice would interrupt and say, 'Don't do that, Brianne. Just let Me love you. Let Me help you. Spend some time with Me and remember I died to set you free, not chain you to a bunch of expectations you can't possibly do perfectly all the time. Do your best, but let Me fill in the gaps and make it all okay."

She had been listening to that Voice more and more, and she did feel she was learning to delight in God. But tonight she realized Danielle's secret to her quick recovery. She had learned to simply delight in God, allowing Him to forgive her and restore her and set her completely free.

Danielle wasn't here because it was the right thing to do or because she was trying to prove anything. She was here because she wanted to be. Because she loved God and wanted to enjoy Him and the life He had designed for her.

And Brianne wanted to be that way too.

Chapter Eight

When Brianne hadn't heard anything from her dad by the end of February about the possibility of Pastor Doug stepping down as the youth pastor and hiring someone new, she decided to let him know she had overheard him telling her mom about it and wanted to know what was going on.

Even though Austin's family wouldn't be moving, Brianne still wanted Pastor Doug as her youth pastor. No matter what he thought of himself, she knew he was doing a great job, and she wondered if he needed to hear she and many of the other kids felt the same way.

When her dad came home from work on Friday, she was outside on the porch waiting for him. She asked if she could talk to him for a minute, and he sat down beside her.

"What's up, sweetheart?"

"Do you remember when I said if things between me and Austin changed I would tell you about it?"

"Yes."

"Well," she said, dragging it out as if she had something significant to tell him, "they haven't."

The tense look that had come over his face melted away, and he shook his head. "You are enjoying this turning-thirteen thing way too much."

"I know. Don't you love me?"

"Yes, I do," he said, giving her a kiss on the forehead. "Do you really have something you want to talk about, or can I go take my heart medication now?"

She told him she knew about Pastor Doug and was wondering if anything more had been decided.

"I've been praying about it and so has Pastor Doug. At this point we think trying to bring someone new in when we're still finishing the new building might be a mistake, so we're going to wait until then, at least. I was anxious to get Doug hired on full-time, and I know we could do that, but bringing in someone new will be a more involved process."

"Are you mad I was listening?"

"No. And if anything significant was happening, I would have told you about it. Why didn't you ask me about this right away?"

She shrugged. "I was scared the Lockharts might be moving. In a way, I didn't want to know."

"Oh, I see."

She smiled. "I guess you could say Austin is my best friend now, and I can't lose two best friends in one year."

"I understand, sweetheart, but don't try to handle things yourself. If something's bothering you, or you need to talk, I want you to come to me or your mom. Don't keep secrets or think we're keeping secrets from you. We're a family. Families share things, not hide them."

"Okay," she said.

"What else? I can see there's something going on behind those hazel eyes."

She admitted it. "I'm getting scared we're going to move again. Last time I knew about it three weeks before we left. I need more time than that now."

He pulled her close and held her in his arms. "I know."

"Do you think that might happen anytime soon?"

"I can't make you any promises, Brianne, but I can say things are going well right now, and I would be surprised if God moved us on within the next year or two."

"And if that changes, you'll let me know?"

"Yes, I will."

"Thanks, Daddy."

"I love you, sweetheart. You know that, right?"

"Yes. I love you too."

"What did you help your mom make for dinner tonight?"

"Actually, the boys are helping her."

"Ah, it must be pizza night."

"Yes."

"Sounds good. Let's go have some."

With a much lighter heart, Brianne stood from her spot on the top step, and her dad followed her to the front door.

"You should call Austin and invite him over tonight."

"Why?"

"It's Friday. You've gone over there several times. He took you to the concert. It's your turn."

"You wouldn't mind?"

"Why would I mind? Sarah used to come over every other day."

"Would you rather go pick him up or take him home?"

"Either, or both."

"Okay," she said, stepping inside. "Can he sleep over too?"

She got tickled for that.

***

Brianne called Austin after dinner to see if he could come over and watch a movie with her and her family. He said he wanted to, and she went with her dad to go pick him up. They returned to the house and were about to start the movie when the phone rang. Her mom answered it, telling them to go ahead and start, but when Brianne heard it was for her, she got up from where she was sitting on the couch beside Austin and asked them to wait.

"Who is it?" she asked her mom on the way to the phone.

"Ashlee."

Brianne wondered why Ashlee would be calling her. They hadn't been talking much lately. Not because Brianne was avoiding her, but because Ashlee had only been at church on Sunday mornings since she had joined a junior swim team in January. The meets were on Thursdays, and they only had one class together this semester instead of two, and it was social studies where she didn't sit by her.

"Hello?"

"Hi, Brianne. It's Ashlee. How are you?"

"Fine. How are you?"

"Great! I was calling you to invite you to my birthday party next Friday. Do you think you can come?"

"I don't know," she said, feeling surprised Ashlee would be inviting her, especially after what had happened last year. "What time?"

"We're going to be meeting at my house at six-thirty and we're going to the mall to have makeovers and our picture taken—you know the kind that make you look like a model. And then we're going to the movies, coming back to my house for cake and ice cream at midnight, and everyone's staying over and we'll have breakfast here on Saturday."

"I'll have to ask," she said. "Can I tell you on Sunday?"

"Yeah, sure. I need to know by Monday at the latest though so my mom can make the right number of makeover appointments."

"Okay, I'll let you know. Thanks for inviting me."

"Of course I'm inviting you. I always do."

"I know. I have to go. We're watching a movie, and everyone is waiting for me."

"Okay, bye."

Brianne hung up the phone and felt a knot forming in her stomach. She really didn't want to go. Hanging around Ashlee at church and youth activities was tolerable, but being with her and a bunch of Ashlee's friends from school wasn't Brianne's idea of a good time.

In fifth grade she had gone to her birthday party at Pizza Playhouse, and it had been okay because Sarah was there too. But last year Ashlee had a swimming and slumber-party, and the swimming had been fun, but once they'd gone back to her house it had become very un-fun.

Sarah hadn't been able to go because her family was doing something. After watching a scary movie, playing Truth or Dare, and then trying to go to sleep while the others were playing pranks on girls who were already sleeping, Brianne was so ready to go home. Then Ashlee decided to sneak out and play a prank on her neighbor. Brianne really didn't want to go through all that again.

Going back into the living room to watch the movie, Brianne knew her mom was watching her to see what kind of a conversation she'd had with Ashlee, but she didn't want to say anything in front of everybody, so she avoided her gaze, hoping her mom would take the hint and wait to ask her about it later. She didn't suppose anyone else even knew who had called.

"Okay, I'm here," she said, sitting beside Austin on the small sofa and pulling Beth onto her lap. "You can start it now."

Her dad did so, and she felt determined to push aside her troubled thoughts and enjoy the movie. It was one she had seen in the theater last summer with Sarah, and she'd really liked it, but it was more of a kids' movie, so Austin hadn't, but she thought he would like it anyway. He tried to act so cool sometimes, but she knew he wasn't much different now than he'd been in fifth grade.

Halfway through the movie, her dad paused the DVD for a bathroom and snack break, and she asked Austin if he liked it so far. He had been laughing at the funny parts, so she knew he did, but she wanted to hear him say so because he'd seemed skeptical when she'd picked it.

"Yeah, it's all right," he said.

"Are you glad you came over?"

"Yes, but are you sure your dad's okay with it? He keeps giving me a look."

She laughed. "Whose idea do you think it was to invite you over?"

"You're not serious."

"Yes, I am. I talked to him about your dad and how I was afraid of you moving, and after we talked he told me I should invite you over instead of me always going over to your house."

"So, why does he keep looking at me?"

"Just to let you know he's watching."

Her dad returned to the room and immediately looked their direction. She started laughing. Besides Steven who was waiting patiently for the movie to continue, they were the only ones in the room.

"All right, what's so funny over here?" he asked, tickling her knee and then passing them by to go to his chair.

"Nothing, Daddy," she said.

"Would you like to have this chair, Austin? It's more comfortable than that old couch."

"No, I'm all right," he said. "I couldn't take your comfortable chair, Pastor Jake."

"No, I'm sure you couldn't. Your mom and dad have raised you better than that, I'm sure."

Her mom returned to the room and handed them a bowl of popcorn. "Are you being good, Jacob Thomas Carmichael?"

"What? I'm just offering Austin my nice comfortable chair over here."

"And he's not taking it? How polite of him."

Brianne was starting to feel embarrassed, but her mom leaned down and whispered something to Austin that neither Brianne nor her dad could hear, and she was very curious to know what it was, especially when Austin laughed.

He left to go use the bathroom when he saw J.T. returning, so she didn't have a chance to ask him, and her mother wasn't about to share the secret, even when her dad pulled her onto his lap and tried to kiss his way into getting it out of her.

The phone rang again, and Brianne went to answer it since her parents were otherwise occupied. This time Brianne was much more excited about the caller and even more excited about the invitation Sarah had for her.

"We're going to California for Spring Break. My dad won this office-pool thing they had at work, and it's for five days at a resort at Lake Tahoe. Do you want to go?"

Chapter Nine

After Brianne got all the details from Sarah about the trip, she told her they were watching a movie and she needed to go but said she would talk to her mom and dad and call her back tomorrow.

"If you can't go, don't worry about it. But I'd really love it if you could."

"And I'd love to say yes right now, but I'm not sure if we have anything planned for that week."

Brianne returned to the living room and sat beside Austin. She wasn't sure if she should say anything and hold up the movie, but her mom asked who had called.

She told them everything, and she wasn't surprised when her mom and dad looked at each other and her dad said, "We'll talk about it."

After everyone else had turned their attention back to the movie, Austin leaned over and whispered, "You are so going."

She smiled but wondered how he knew that, or at least thought he knew. She couldn't tell anything by her parents' reaction. But he was right. She didn't say anything more about it to her mom and dad that night, but when she asked them in the morning, they said they had talked about it and decided it was fine.

She called Sarah to tell her, and she also told her about Ashlee's party, saying she didn't really want to go but felt like maybe she should.

"Talk to your mom and dad and see what they think," Sarah suggested. "Maybe they'll say you can't because of what happened last year and then you'll have the perfect excuse."

Remembering what her dad had said to her yesterday about coming to them when she had a problem or something was bothering her, she knew Sarah was right, but she wanted to know what Sarah would do if it was her.

"I'd talk to my mom and dad first, but if they left it up to me then I'd have to pray about it and see what God was telling me to do."

"And if you felt like He was telling you to go?"

"Then I'd trust Him to take care of me and have a reason for wanting me there. That's what I've done with moving here. It was hard at first, and I still miss you a lot, but He is taking care of me. Every time I see Ryan, I'm reminded of that."

"Is he still the only close friend you have?"

"Pretty much. I'm getting to know some of the others slowly, but me and Ryan connected right from the beginning like me and you, and I know that's God. It's the only explanation."

Brianne knew God had done the same thing for her when she first moved here two years ago. In Sweet Home she'd had several good friends, but all of those relationships had come about slowly. But Sarah had been there right from the start when she most needed a new friend, and now He'd done the same thing with Austin, having their friendship ready to go to a whole new level when Sarah had moved away. She hadn't done anything to gain Austin's friendship. It was simply there.

When she hung up the phone, she decided to call Austin to let him know he had been right about her parents letting her go to Lake Tahoe with Sarah.

"How did you know that?" she asked.

"What reason would they have to say no? She's your best friend. They know her mom and dad really well and know they'll take good care of you. They know how much you miss her. And you've never done anything to make them distrust you and think you would get into some kind of trouble when you're away from them for a week."

She almost asked him for advice about Ashlee's party too, but she decided to talk to her mom and dad first. After she let him go, saying she would see him at band practice later, she went to look for her mom and found her in her bedroom, hanging up some clothes. Her dad had taken her brothers to the skate park. Brianne told her about Ashlee's invitation and waited for her response.

"Did Ashlee ask you last night when she called?"

"Yes."

"I thought you looked upset about something."

"I wasn't upset, I just felt like I didn't want to go, but I don't know how to tell her without making her mad."

"Do you want me to say you can't so that can be your excuse?"

"I don't know. I feel like I should go since she invited me. I've been trying to not hold things against her she's done to me in the past, but if I don't go, I feel like that's what I'm doing."

"How long do you have to decide?"

"I need to let her know by Monday, but if she's at church tomorrow, she'll probably be expecting an answer because I told her I'd just have to ask."

"Why do you not want to go?"

"She acts different at school and around her friends than she does at church. She pretty much ignores me if any of her other friends are around. And going to have a makeover isn't really my thing. Ashlee usually picks scary movies I don't like, and I hate playing Truth or Dare, and that's Ashlee's favorite game. She loves to humiliate people, and she's really good at it with me."

Her mom came over to give her a hug, and Brianne let the tears fall. She had the same thought she'd had many times before: *Why couldn't Ashlee have moved away instead of Sarah?*

"You know, sweetie," her mom said, "I know you've forgiven Ashlee, and that's great. Maybe going to her party will say, 'I forgive you and want to be your friend.' But maybe not going could let her know she can't treat people that way and expect to have any friends worth having. I think she invited you because she knows you're a good friend to have, even if she won't admit that or doesn't act like it."

"So, you don't think I should go?"

"I think you need to do what's best for you. If you feel strong enough to go, then go, and I'm sure you'll be fine. But if you don't, God's not going to be pointing a finger at you and saying, 'You're not loving her like you should.' He knows, and He understands. Only He can give us the capacity to love people who have hurt us, and if you don't feel ready, then go to Him and say, 'I'm not ready. I want to love her more, but I'm not there yet.'"

Her mom had finished with her laundry, and Brianne asked if she could use the phone in her room. "I talked to Sarah about it, and she gave me some good advice, but I want to ask Austin too. He usually tells me things I haven't thought of before."

Her mom gave her permission to use the phone, and once she left the room, Brianne said a brief prayer, asking God to help her make this decision, and then she called Austin. She caught him as he was about to head out the door, his mom told her.

"Hi. Me again," she said. "If you need to go, this can wait."

"I'm in no hurry," he said. "What's up? You can't decide if you want to take your pink bathing suit to Tahoe or your purple one?"

She laughed. "Actually I'm going to have to get a new one. I've grown about three inches since last summer, and my body—well, we won't go there."

He didn't say anything, but she could picture his face, and she laughed. "Sorry. Sometimes I forget you're not Sarah."

"On second thought, I would like to get to the skate park before dark—"

"Oh, is that where you're going? My dad is there with my brothers right now."

"Okay, I'm listening," he said. "Tell me all about what you're going shopping for this afternoon."

She got serious then and told him the real reason for her call. He sounded surprised she was asking him. "I asked Sarah and my mom, and they both gave me things to think about, but I'm wondering what you think? Do you think it would be a huge mistake for me to go, or would you be disappointed in me if I didn't?"

"Why does it matter what I think?"

"Because you're my friend, and I value your opinion. And because sometimes I feel like you know me better than I know myself. If there's one thing I've learned about our friendship during the last six months, that's it."

"What did your mom and Sarah say?"

"I'm not telling you. I want your opinion, Austin. Honestly. Whatever you're thinking, I want to hear it."

"I think you should go, but on your terms, not hers."

"What do you mean?"

"When you talk to her at church in the morning, you should ask her what movie they're going to see, and if it's something you know you won't like, then you say, 'I can't go if that's what you're going to see.'"

"And if she says they are anyway?"

"Then you're saying no because of the movie, not because of her. The makeover thing might not be you, but you can tolerate it. But a scary movie—that's different because she's asking you to be a part of something you don't like."

"Do you honestly think she might change her mind?"

"I don't know. I bet no one has ever challenged her before."

"Austin! I can't do that. She'll eat me alive."

"Maybe, but I'll be close by to defend you."

"You will?"

"Sure. If you ask her with other people around, she'll be more likely to back down."

"And if she changes her mind about the movie but then keeps me up half the night playing games I hate?"

"Just don't play. She can't force you to. Take a book and read, or listen to music and say you'd rather not play. There's a difference between being a friend and sometimes doing what she likes to do, and being walked all over. It's okay to stand up to her and not always play by her rules. That's being a friend in a different kind of way. It's for her own good to have a friend like that."

Brianne knew what he was saying, but she wasn't sure she was strong enough to be that way with Ashlee. She thought about what her mom had said and knew she was going to have to pray about it and then do what she felt God leading her to do, but at the same time not get down on herself if she couldn't be that kind of friend to Ashlee yet.

"Will you pray for me?"

"Yes, and I'll say one more thing."

"What?"

"If you decide to go, ask your dad if you can borrow his cell phone to take with you—like for an emergency in case Ashlee ends up changing the plan and you need to be able to call him so he can come pick you up, and then I'll call you like every hour just to make sure you're okay."

That plan made her smile. "You will?"

"Sure. If I was a girl, I'd have you get me invited to the party too so we could hang out together if Ashlee ends up ignoring you most of the time, but since I'm not, I'll be there with you in a different way."

"You're so smart. How do you come up with this stuff?"

"Well, you prayed about it and then called to ask me for advice. Did you think God was really going to answer you?"

"You mean like when I asked Him for a good friend after Sarah moved?"

"Is that how I ended up being your friend? I always did feel like it was against my will."

She laughed. "God can only use those who are willing to be used. That's what my dad says."

"Okay, so maybe it's not so bad."

"Having a girl for a best friend?"

"If that girl is you? Definitely not."

Chapter Ten

Before Brianne left her parents' room, she decided to call Emily and Marissa to see if they were going to Ashlee's party. If either of them were, she knew she would feel much better about going. But she doubted it because Marissa and Ashlee hadn't been getting along too well lately. And Emily hadn't gone last year because her parents wouldn't let her.

"I didn't get invited," Emily said.

"And I have no idea why she invited me. If you were going, I'd feel better about it, but I don't really know any of her friends from school."

"Are you going?"

"I don't know. I'm trying to decide. Consider yourself blessed you didn't get asked."

Emily laughed. "Okay, I will."

"Did you send in your camp registration?"

"Yes. For the last week in August, right?"

"Yep. I sent in mine and so did Sarah and Austin. I can't wait!"

They talked for a little while longer, but Emily had limits on how long she could be on the phone, and Brianne didn't want to get her into trouble. She also didn't want to be in here too much longer and have her mom think she had been talking to Austin this whole time.

She went to use the phone in the kitchen to call Marissa, and she saw her mom was outside in the backyard with Beth. It had been sunny the last few days, and Brianne was anxious to get outside herself, but she called Marissa first. Her response was the same as Emily's.

"I didn't get invited, and honestly, I'm glad."

"I have no idea why she invited me."

"I know why."

"Why?"

"Because you actually talk to her. Why do you do that?"

"Because God tells me to. I want to hate her, but I can't."

"I don't hate her. I just can't stand to be around her for very long. Especially since she's all buddy-buddy with Caitlin again. They're in my P.E. class this semester, and they both like the same guy. The same thing is going to happen that happened with Brady last year. Why do they do that?"

"Who knows?"

She asked Marissa about camp too, but she hadn't sent her registration form in yet. She wanted to go but wasn't sure about her family's plans for the summer. They didn't plan much in advance, but her parents loved to go places.

"You could always send it in and then change your mind later," she suggested. "And if you can't afford the deposit money, the church would pay it for you."

"They would? I thought we could only earn the rest of it?"

"Well, that's true, but there's a scholarship fund. Like if I wanted to invite someone who didn't go to church and they couldn't afford it but they weren't around to memorize Bible verses and help with the fundraisers, they could still go. My dad and Pastor Doug never want money to be the reason someone can't go to camp and stuff."

"The church already paid for me to go on that retreat last time."

"Yeah, so?"

"And they would pay for me to go to camp too?"

"Well, yeah."

"What's that mean?"

"Nothing."

"No, there's something you're not telling me. You earned part of the money for me, didn't you?"

"Why do you think that?"

"Because I know they can't pay for anyone's friend who wants to come. Ashlee would be bringing her whole crew every time."

"Okay, yeah. If we want to bring a friend and they can't pay, then we have to earn part of their money— not all, but at least some."

"And you were going to do that with this, weren't you? Tell me the church would pay my deposit, but you would be earning it for me?"

"Yes. I want you to go, Mar. And if you can't because your family is doing something else, that's fine, but if you can't because you didn't get your registration in on time or you can't afford the deposit money, I'd hate to see that happen."

"Brianne, how can you and Ashlee know the same God and be so different? Ashlee wouldn't even want me there, let alone pay for me to go."

"I don't know. Maybe she doesn't really know Him. I mean, I know she knows about Him, but she doesn't have His love in her heart. At least it doesn't seem like it."

"Like I should talk," Marissa said. "I'm not really loving her either."

"It's hard. I'm not sure I would pay for Ashlee to go either."

"I think you would. You're just that way. No matter who it is. How can I be more like that?"

Brianne honestly didn't know. She didn't know why she was that way. She had no idea why she was concerned about hurting Ashlee's feelings if she didn't go to her ridiculous birthday party. Last year it would have been more about Ashlee being mad at her, but that wasn't it this time, she realized. She couldn't care less if Ashlee got mad. But she cared about her.

If Marissa hadn't asked her that question, she probably would have let it be a mystery, but since Marissa wanted to know how she could love girls like Ashlee, and Brianne wanted to know herself, she told her she didn't know but she would ask.

When her dad got home later and he had a free minute, she asked him, telling him what Marissa had said and the difference she'd noticed in her own heart toward Ashlee compared to last year. "Why do we love some people more than others, and why do we love even when people have hurt us?"

Her dad got up from the couch where they were sitting to get his Bible from beside his chair. He turned to the book of First John, and he read some words to her from Chapter Four, verse 16:

"We know how much God loves us, and we have put our trust in him. God is love, and all who live in love, live in God, and God lives in them."

Brianne waited for him to explain it, but she could see what she had said to Marissa about Ashlee not really knowing God could be right.

"You believe God loves you, Brianne. You believe He made you and Jesus came to die for you, right?"

"Yes."

"When we do that, God's love becomes a part of us. Jesus is in our hearts, and He is love, so it's impossible to have Him in there and not love. There's lots of different degrees of love, and we naturally love some people more than others because if they're loving us, it's easier for us to love them. But God can help us to love in a supernatural way—the way He does. You can't love someone like Ashlee on your own, but God loves her, and that love becomes a part of your heart when you are close to Him."

"But why does Marissa have more trouble loving her than me? She knows Jesus too."

"Or why do you love her more now than you did last year, even though she's been worse to you this year than ever before?"

"Yeah. What's up with that? Why can't I just stop being her friend!"

Her dad laughed. "Wouldn't that be nice? There have been some people in my life I'd like to forget about."

"Really?"

"I'm human just like you, sweetheart."

"But we can't forget about them because God doesn't?"

"Yeah. Pretty much. Although it's not just about them, it's about us too. He knows we're happier when we love people than when we don't, and so He gives us that ability. And the more you believe in His love for you, the more you are able to love others."

"Do you think Ashlee even knows God?"

"I never like to say what's in other people's hearts. Only God can know that. But I don't think Ashlee really grasps God's love for her. She might know about Jesus in her head and believe in a mental way, but I don't think it's reached her heart. If it had, she wouldn't be so anxious to please a bunch of friends who don't care about her half as much as you do."

"Do you think that's why she invited me to her party? Deep down she knows I really care about her?"

"Yes."

Brianne let out a fake cry and hugged him around the neck. "Why me?"

He laughed softly. "I have a feeling you're going to end up with a lot of Ashlees in your life, so you'd better get used to it. God won't waste a heart like yours."

Brianne felt a unique sense of peace come over her with her dad's words, and somehow going to Ashlee's party didn't seem like such a big deal. If Ashlee ignored her or made fun of her, so what? She didn't need Ashlee to be her friend. She had her family and her own perfectly nice friends. She didn't need Ashlee, but Ashlee needed her.

In the morning when Ashlee asked if she could come, she said yes, but she did ask what movie they were going to see. There was a scary movie out right now that was rated PG-13. When Ashlee said they were thinking of that one but hadn't decided for sure, she said, "My mom and dad don't want me to see that, so is it okay if we don't?"

"Yeah, sure. We'll pick something else. Me and Caitlin have already seen it anyway."

"Okay, thanks. I'm glad you invited me. It seems like I hardly see you anymore."

"I know."

"Are you going to camp this summer?"

"I'm still thinking about it."

"Don't wait too long, or you might not get in."

"Okay. I have the registration form at home. I'll send it in this week."

"We're doing a babysitting fundraiser here next Saturday, and we've already had a lot of parents sign up to bring their kids, so we should get some good money out of that."

"Okay. I'll be here. Remind me."

"I will."

Brianne hadn't made a point of making sure Austin was close by when she talked to Ashlee, but apparently he'd been watching for when Ashlee came to talk to her because when Ashlee turned to leave, she watched her go and then heard Austin's voice in her ear.

"Impressive, Brianne. That was so smooth."

She turned around and laughed. "Where did you come from?"

"I was just using my invisible cloak here," he said, putting on his jacket.

"Why doesn't it make you invisible now?"

"It's magic. I can make it work when I want it to."

Brianne noticed Austin's hair was getting long again. He had thin hair that was a darker shade of blonde like hers, but the ends turned lighter and curled slightly when it began to hang below his ears. He had worn it that way in fifth grade, but last year he'd gotten it cut when she and Sarah had made a comment about how cute it was. Austin didn't want to be cute. He wanted to be cool, so he'd had it cut really short.

"I think you should leave your hair that way," she said. "I like it."

"Shut up. I'm getting it cut tomorrow."

"Don't. You have great hair, Austin. I'm serious. Leave it."

"Seriously?"

"Yes. Maybe cut it in the back a little, but leave the sides covering your ears. It's a good look for you."

He smiled at her in a way he did once in awhile, a way that made her wish she was sixteen and didn't have to wait three more years to have him as more than a friend.

"What made you decide to go to Ashlee's party?" he asked, getting back to the subject.

Brianne wanted to go see if her mom needed her help with children's church today, so she invited Austin to walk with her. She told him what Sarah had said about trusting God to be with her, and what her mom and dad had said about Ashlee needing her friendship.

"And then I kept remembering what you said about not having to always play by her rules, and I decided it's time I start doing that."

Chapter Eleven

Brianne felt good about her decision all week and didn't feel anxious about Ashlee's party until Thursday afternoon when Ashlee came to find her right before she needed to go catch the bus. Ashlee's message was brief but disappointing, especially since Ashlee had told her yesterday what movie they had decided to see and Brianne had been happy with her selection.

"I just wanted to let you know we all decided to invite some guys to meet us at the movies. I asked Kirk Jones."

"Who's that?"

"He's a ninth grader who's on my swim team."

"Do your mom and dad know?"

Ashlee laughed. "No, of course not. That's why they're meeting us there."

"Why are you telling me?"

"Because I thought you might want to ask Silas, or whoever you like right now. I have to run because my mom is picking me up to go shopping for the party. See you tomorrow."

Austin had been standing nearby, waiting for Ashlee to leave. Brianne saw him after she ran off. She turned back to get the rest of what she needed for tonight out of her locker, but she couldn't think straight. Now what was she supposed to do? It was Ashlee's party, so she couldn't tell her not to invite some guy to meet her at the movie theater, but the thought of Ashlee and her friends all having dates and her going alone didn't settle well with her. Did that mean she shouldn't go?

"What was that about?" Austin asked once she had her things together and they were walking toward the outside doors.

"Ashlee and her friends invited a bunch of guys to meet them at the movies, and she wanted to tell me I could bring a date too."

"Cool," he said, putting his arm around her shoulder. "What are we going to see?"

She shoved him away playfully. "It's not funny! Now what am I supposed to do?"

"Tell your mom and dad and see what they say."

"Why do I feel like I'm always running to my parents?" she whined.

"That's what they're there for, Brianne."

"Maybe I shouldn't tell them and just go. What does it matter if I'm the only one without a date? It will only be at the theater anyway."

"Unless they decide to go someplace else for two hours."

Brianne didn't say anything until they were on the bus and neither did Austin. She was about to go home, call Ashlee's house, and leave her a message she couldn't go tomorrow night after all, but Austin repeated his words from before.

"I think you should ask me to meet you there."

"And not tell my parents?"

"No. We'll tell them. I'll have my dad drive me, and if Ashlee and everyone stays there and watches the movie and it's all harmless, then we'll sit together and I'll go home afterwards while you go back to Ashlee's house. But if they all decide to see a different movie or go someplace else, you won't have to stay there and sit through a movie all by yourself. And, if you're having a terrible time, my dad can take you home."

Brianne smiled. "If Ashlee sees you there, she will freak out!"

"She said you could invite whoever you want."

"She hates you so much."

"That's because she can't get me to fall down and kiss her feet like most guys."

"Why is that?"

"I've known her since we were both in diapers. She was bossy and annoying at three, and I never did what she said. She's hated me ever since, and I haven't cried any tears over it. If she doesn't want to speak to me, then fine with me."

"But you want *me* to go to her party and be her friend?"

"No, you want to do that."

"What! You were the one who told me I should go when I had almost decided not to!"

"No, I told you if you were going to go, you should go on your terms, not hers. To be a friend but not let her walk all over you."

"And that's what you do in your own unique way?"

"I try. But I think you can do it better than me. I annoy her too much. You can be more—sneaky about it."

"Like she would never expect me to actually bring someone, especially you, so that's what I should do?"

"If your mom and dad say it's okay, and mine too, of course."

"And you think they will?"

"We won't know if we don't ask."

"I'll think about it," she said. "Right now I'm thinking of calling and saying I'm not coming."

"Whatever you want to do. I'm just offering."

"Offering what? To be my boyfriend for the night? Ashlee will have a hay-day with that one."

"Like I care what Ashlee thinks about me and you."

Brianne didn't respond to that. Maybe Austin didn't care, but she did. Not because Ashlee would make it out to be like she and Austin were an item now, but more so because she would take their very sincere and close friendship and drag it through the mud, turning it into some stupid junior high romance that would be yesterday's news by next week. She didn't want to be put into the same category as Ashlee and Brady, or Caitlin and Brady, or Jillene and Brady, or Caitlin and Danny, or Ashlee and Kirk—whoever that was.

When she got home, she didn't waste any time dumping the latest development on her mom, who didn't seem too surprised at the news.

"What do you want to do?" she asked.

"Not go."

"You don't have to, honey. I'll call Mrs. Moore myself and tell her we've decided to not let you go. I can say, 'I didn't realize there were going to be boys meeting the girls at the movies, and we don't allow Brianne to do that yet.'"

Brianne wanted to have her mom do that so badly, or make the call herself and say she couldn't come without explaining why, but Austin's idea remained on her mind, and she decided to mention it to her mom, just to see what she would say.

Her mom listened, and when she finished, a slight smile formed on her face. "That was Austin's idea?"

"Yes."

"Do you want to do that?"

"I don't know. In a way, I guess. Austin's really smart about stuff like this. I never realized how much he watches people and figures them out. He knows more about me than I do, and he definitely knows more about Ashlee than anyone I've ever met."

Her mom laughed. "Let me talk to your dad about it. I like the idea of bringing Pastor Doug in on this. At least Ashlee pretends to respect him. Having Austin there might make her realize she's not hiding as much as she thinks."

Brianne went to her room to do her homework. She had a ton tonight and also had youth group. She was able to get it all done by dinnertime, but her mind kept wandering to what she would do tomorrow. She tried to figure out what she wanted her parents to say.

When Daddy came home and her mom told him about Austin's idea, what did she hope his response was?

'No way. She's not going.'?

'She can go, but I don't want Austin meeting her there.'?

'She can go as long as Austin meets her there.'?

'Okay, I think we need to move now and get our daughter away from Ashlee and Austin!'?

She smiled at the last possibility. Not because she wanted to move, but because she knew her dad was trying very hard to accept the fact her best friend was a boy, but it wasn't easy for him.

Of the other three, she supposed there would be advantages and disadvantages to each of them. If she didn't go, she could avoid the whole thing, but Ashlee might be mad. If she went and was the only girl without a date, that could be awkward and embarrassing, but she would be showing Ashlee and the other girls she didn't need to have a boyfriend right now. And if Austin met her there, she knew she would like that, and it would probably be the highlight of the entire party for her. But it might give Ashlee the wrong idea, and they would never hear the end of it, or Ashlee would be mad she had told anyone else they were meeting guys there, especially the youth pastor and his son.

Okay, Jesus. What am I supposed to do? I'm willing to do whatever my parents think is best, but if they leave it up to me, help! I never thought growing up would be this complicated. I thought life would get easier, not harder. I don't know if I'm ready to be a teenager. I'm glad I've decided not to date until I'm sixteen because I can't imagine adding that to everything else right now. Even with just having Austin as a friend, I find myself having to carefully balance my time between him and everyone else. I need him to be my best friend, but he can't be my only friend. I need Sarah and Marissa and Emily and Brooke and Danielle and Silas and even Ashlee, just in different ways.

She was about to go help her mom set the table for dinner when she heard a soft knock on her door. She invited whomever it was to come in, and it was her dad. She hadn't heard him come home, and she didn't know if her mom had talked to him already or not.

"Hi, Daddy. I didn't know you were here."

"I just got home," he said, closing the door behind him. "Can I sit down?"

"Sure," she said, moving her books out of the way and putting them into her backpack. When she looked up at him, he had a concerned look on his face, and she waited for him to speak.

"How are you feeling about going to Ashlee's party tomorrow?"

"Did you talk to Mom?"

"Just for a minute. She said I should come talk to you about it—that you have something to tell me? And before you say anything, I want you to know I'm not having a real good feeling about you going. I don't know why, I've just had a bad feeling all day."

Brianne had expected her mom to tell her dad about the latest development, for them to talk about it, and then tell her what they thought. She hadn't planned on having to tell her dad directly about Ashlee turning this into secret-date night and Austin's willingness to be her "date." But she didn't have a choice now.

"I was feeling fine about it until today after school," she answered honestly.

"What happened after school?"

"Ashlee told me she and all the other girls have asked different guys to meet them at the movie theater. She asked some ninth-grader she knows from her swim team, but her parents don't know about it, and she told me I could ask someone to meet me there too. If I don't, I'll be the only one without a date."

"And that's what you're concerned about? Not having a date like everyone else?"

"No. That doesn't bother me except most of the guys I won't know, or I do, but I don't really like them; and the thought of being alone there without any of my close friends makes me uncomfortable, especially after I talked to Austin about it and he thinks they might not even stay at the theater if her parents aren't going to be there."

"You could call me if that happens."

"I know, and I would never be stupid enough go someplace else, so I was thinking I could go and see what happens and call you if I need to, or not go at all, but then Austin had another idea, and I think this is what Mom wanted you to come talk to me about."

"Let me guess. Austin wants to be your date?"

She smiled. "How did you know that?"

He laughed.

"What?"

"Your mom is real funny, and Austin—that kid is big trouble."

"Daddy, you're making no sense."

"I guess your mom hasn't told you the story of our first date, huh?"

What did her mom and dad have to do with this? "I know she let you kiss her even though she had only known you for a week."

"Do you know why she went out with me in the first place?"

"No."

He sighed and shook his head like he couldn't believe he was going to tell her this. She turned more to face him, and he told her the story.

"At the end of her second year of college, your mom had this guy who liked her and kept asking her to go out with him, but she didn't want to and kept telling him no. And then at the beginning of her junior year she saw him on the first day of classes, and he said he'd been thinking about her all summer and asked her to go out with him again.

"Your mom was very upset by it because she was tired of him always trying to talk to her and not taking no for an answer, and the first time I met her she was sitting behind me in a class we had together, and I could tell she was upset, so after class I asked her if she was all right.

"At first she said she was fine, but I walked out with her and we were headed in the same direction, and so I asked her again—"

Her mom stepped into the room, hearing the last phrase he had spoken, and she interrupted him. "He said, 'If you're all right, then why are those beautiful green eyes so red today?'"

Brianne laughed.

"Yes, okay," her dad admitted. "That's what I said. Do you want to tell this story?"

"Oh, no. I think our daughter needs to hear it straight from you, but don't leave anything out."

Her mom stepped back out, saying dinner was ready whenever they were, and then her dad reluctantly continued. "I figured out real fast it was going to take more than charming lines to get her to talk to me, but I was honestly concerned, so I told her that, and then she told me everything—I think she was trying to tell me she'd had it with guys who wouldn't leave her alone, more so than she actually trusted me, but once I knew, I told her I would talk to the guy if she wanted, and she was desperate enough to take me up on it.

"So, I met her for lunch the next day, and she pointed him out, and it was actually someone I knew, so I went to talk to him and told him to stop bothering my girlfriend."

"Daddy! You lied?"

"It wasn't really a lie. I told him that we were "together", because at that moment we were having lunch, and then I asked him to stop asking her out. I never actually said she was my girlfriend, but he assumed that's what I meant."

"Did Mom know that?"

"Yes, I told her, and then I said, 'Maybe we should have lunch here together every day this week so he actually believes I'm your boyfriend,' and she said, 'Okay,' so that's what we did for the next two days, and on Thursday I asked her out for real—actually that's not quite true. I was teasing her because the guy was watching us, and I said, 'I'm not sure he believes you're really my girlfriend, maybe I should kiss you,' and she looked me right in the eye and said, 'I'm not wasting my first kiss on you just to get him to leave me alone.'"

Her dad paused, seeming to smile at the memory of that moment with her mom.

"And what did you say?"

"There had been other things your mom said or did during the time I spent with her that made me want to spend more time with her and take her out for real, but when she told me she'd never kissed anyone, I knew she wasn't just a pretty girl I liked, but she was the one I had been waiting for."

Chapter Twelve

"What did you say?" Brianne repeated.

Daddy laughed. "I said, 'You know, Debbie, as soon as I stop having lunch with you, he's going to be right back over here, so we should go out on Saturday and then maybe you can kiss me without it being a waste.'"

Brianne smiled. She tried to picture her mom and dad being so young and first meeting each other, and she could almost picture it. She could imagine her dad saying that.

"That's how I knew what Austin said to you," her dad went on. "And this isn't the first time I've seen myself in him."

"But Austin isn't trying to be my boyfriend for real."

"I know, but he's doing the same thing. I honestly wanted to protect your mom from having to deal with guys like that anymore. I had other hopes, but that was my primary reason for asking her out. And I don't know what Austin is thinking or what hopes he may have for the future, but I do believe he's being honest about wanting to be there tomorrow so he can protect you from whatever might happen and give you a couple of hours of honest fun with someone you enjoy spending time with."

"And you're okay with that?"

"Sure. I trust Austin, and I trust you, sweetheart. But I don't trust Ashlee, and if you're going, I would feel a lot better if I knew Austin was there too."

"Yeah, me too," she said, suddenly realizing God was already answering her prayer about being with her tomorrow night and helping her through this. And she never would have imagined Him doing so in this way.

"Come here," her dad said, opening his arms and inviting her into them. He'd done so in the past when she had gotten into trouble for something and he'd come to her room to talk about it and tell her what her punishment would be, but he had always ended that time with a hug and let her know he loved her very much. This time she wasn't in trouble, but she needed the comfort of his arms just the same.

"And you can trust God too, Daddy. That's what I'm going to do. With or without Austin there, I still need Jesus to get me through this."

"And He will," her dad said, kissing the top of her head. "I love you very, very much, but He loves you even more."

Her dad called Pastor Doug after dinner, and he talked to Austin too. When he had finished, he passed the phone over to her, but since she was going to be seeing Austin at youth group in thirty minutes, they didn't talk long.

Austin waited until after youth group when she was waiting for her dad to come pick her up before mentioning it again. They had decided not to tell anyone he was going to be meeting her there tomorrow, so he hadn't had a chance to say anything until now.

"I'm surprised your dad made up his mind so fast."

She smiled. "There's a story behind it, but I want to wait and tell you when we have more time."

"Tomorrow night?"

"I don't know, maybe. But that might not be the best place."

"Did your mom and dad know each other when they were kids?"

"No, they met in college."

"Your dad said something to me on the phone about how I remind him of himself when he was young, and then in the background I heard your mom say, 'Yeah, me too.' What was that about?"

"It's a part of the story, but my dad wasn't talking about when he was thirteen, he was talking about when he was twenty."

"Is that a good thing?"

"Yeah, I think it's a good thing."

"Oh, man, this is going to be tough."

"What?"

"I'm not even dating you yet, and I'm already—. Never mind."

"Austin!" She laughed. "You're already what?"

"Scared, Brianne. Scared out of my—."

Marissa came over to say good night to them, and Austin didn't finish his thought. She and Miguel had

113

been talking to Pastor Doug afterwards, and they were the last two there besides them.

"See you tomorrow," Marissa said. "Are you still going to Ashlee's party?"

"Yes," she said. "Pray for me."

"I will. Smile pretty for the pictures."

Brianne hadn't forgotten about that, and she had been feeling sort of indifferent about getting a makeover and having pictures taken, but she suddenly realized when Austin met her at the theater tomorrow, she would look very different than he was used to. Most of the time she didn't wear any makeup at all. Maybe she could go into the bathroom and wash it off before he got there if she looked too ridiculous.

She saw her dad's car pull into the parking lot from the youth room window, and Austin walked her out. Once they were in the hallway, she asked him about his earlier comment. "What are you scared of? My dad?"

"He's not just your dad. He's my pastor, and my dad's best friend and his boss. If I mess this up, I am going to be in so much trouble."

She laughed. "You're not going to mess it up. You're too smart for that."

"Don't be too quick to say that, Brianne."

"What's the worst that could happen?"

"Don't even get me started. We'll be here all night."

"Top five fears tomorrow night," she whispered since she could hear Pastor Doug following them out. "Tell me."

114

Austin didn't commit to that, and Brianne felt Pastor Doug come up behind both of them and put his arms around their shoulders. "Isn't God the greatest?"

Brianne looked up and mirrored his wide smile. She didn't have to ask to know something exciting had just happened. She had been wondering what Marissa and Miguel had been talking to him about, and she assumed it must be good.

"What happened?" Austin asked.

"They both want to get baptized. Miguel asked for God's forgiveness tonight while he was up there on stage playing bass. He said one of the songs really spoke to him, and he realized his life is pretty much meaningless right now except for what He's learning and believing about God."

"You can't leave us, Pastor Doug," Brianne blurted out before she could stop herself.

"You know about that?"

"Yes. My dad *is* your boss."

"And you think I should take the full-time job?"

"Yes. There's so much good stuff going on right now, and I know once the new building is finished, it's only going to get better."

"Well, I'm still praying about it. But I appreciate the vote of confidence. If I do step down, I'll make sure we get someone good. I promise."

He changed the subject. "So what's this I hear about you asking Austin out on a date tomorrow night?"

"Dad—"

"I'm talking to the lady, Son. Don't interrupt."

Brianne laughed and glanced at Austin. "I figured it was about time."

"Oh, really?" he said.

She laughed. "He's just being a friend, willing to help out a girl in a bit of a crisis."

Pastor Doug stepped over to the car to speak to her dad through the open window, and she went around to the passenger side. Austin followed her and said something before she opened the door.

"Should I dress up tomorrow night?"

"No, why?"

"I thought maybe since you were getting your picture taken, you would be dressed up."

"No. They have clothes for us to change into there. I'll be in jeans and whatever the rest of the time. Although, since the movie is right after that, I'm not sure what my hair and face will look like, so try not to laugh too much, okay?"

"I'm sure you'll look fine. Maybe as pretty as Sarah."

She tried to hit him in the stomach for that, but he defended himself and grabbed her hand. "I'm just teasing," he said. "You know that, right?"

"Yes."

"Brianne?"

She let go of the secret insecure thoughts she was having. "Yes," she said, meaning it more this time.

"You're pretty, Brianne. Just the way you are. Makeup and all that other stuff will make you look different, not better. You can't improve on what I see every day."

116

Chapter Thirteen

Brianne didn't get to her first class on Friday morning before she knew she had made the right decision about asking Austin to meet her at the movie theater tonight. Ashlee was waiting by her locker when she arrived, and she had more information about her ever-developing party plans.

"You don't need to worry about asking anyone to meet you at the movie theater tonight. If you want to, that's fine, but some of the guys who are coming are bringing friends, so I'll set you up with somebody, okay?"

She ran off before Brianne could respond, and the thing that shocked her most was that Ashlee would think she would want to be set up with some guy she didn't know.

"Do you think she's trying to make me like she is, or does she think I'd be fine with that?" she asked Austin on the way to science class.

"It's Ashlee. Who knows? I don't think she even thinks about what she does half the time."

As the day went on, Brianne's concerns shifted from her fears about tonight to Ashlee's state of mind and lack of common sense. Did she honestly think she was going to get away with meeting a ninth-grader at the movies tonight, having a bunch of other guys there, and her parents never finding out about it? Did she want to get caught? Was she doing this to try and get their attention? Brianne knew if she was going to try and do something like this behind her parents' back, she wouldn't be inviting a girl at church whose parents knew her parents, and especially not the pastor's daughter. It made no sense—unless she had some kind of evil plan up her sleeve.

"Do you think she's trying to set me up?" she asked Austin on the way home.

"What do you mean?"

"Like there's going to be stuff happening tonight she hasn't told me about, and her goal is to completely humiliate me in some way?"

"I wouldn't put it past her."

Brianne got queasy at the thought.

"That's what you'll have your dad's phone for."

"But what if she takes it away or there isn't time for me to call?"

"I think you're getting a little dramatic, Brianne. This isn't a movie, it's real life, and I don't think Ashlee is that smart or that cruel. You know what I think she's doing?"

"What?"

"Trying to get you into trouble. Seeing how far you'll go along with her. Can't you hear it when her mom and dad find out about her having guys at her party without asking permission—one girl has a bad experience and tells her mom and dad or whatever, and then they come down on Ashlee, and she says, 'It wasn't just me. All the girls invited someone. Even Brianne.' Mr. Moore would have a field-day with that one. He's always looking for some way to find fault with your dad."

"But why would she do that? I'm never anything but nice to her."

"Because she's jealous of you."

"Ashlee? Jealous of me? I don't think so."

"I do."

"Why?"

"You're good and kind and you don't get into trouble. You're smarter, have a better family, better friends, and you're prettier."

She began to protest the last one, but Austin put his fingers over her lips. "She has to wear all that makeup and spend an hour on her hair in the morning and wear the latest fashions just to look the way you do naturally."

Brianne wasn't too sure about the 'prettier than Ashlee' thing. In her opinion Ashlee was the prettiest girl in the seventh grade at Clatskanie Junior High, but she couldn't argue with the rest.

Ashlee was popular at school and had a following of friends who worshiped her, but the rest of her life was mostly a mess. She wasn't sure what it was with her family, but something wasn't quite right. Her parents were active in the church, and yet mostly all they did was complain and tear her dad down a lot. Maybe they had the same problem as Ashlee with knowing about God but not really knowing Him.

The bus was nearing her stop, so she didn't argue with Austin further. "Well, whatever it is, I'm glad you're going to be there tonight. You make me feel safe, and I think you're a gift from God."

He smiled and tried to tease his way out of the compliment. "Awww. That's the nicest thing any girl has ever said to me."

She smiled but wasn't going to let him get away with it. "You know something I'm learning about God?"

"What?"

"He never answers my prayers the way I think He's going to. His ideas are always better than mine."

Austin stood up to let her into the aisle as the bus pulled to a stop. "See you later," he said.

"Don't be late," she replied.

Getting off the bus, she stepped to the mailbox as usual, and Danielle asked if she was still going to Ashlee's party tonight. Brianne hadn't told anyone about it except Emily, Marissa, and Austin, but Danielle and Silas knew because on the bus yesterday they'd overheard her freaking out about what Ashlee had told her right after school, but they hadn't heard what Austin had said to her about going with her, nor had she talked to either of them about it since.

"She's going, but Austin's meeting her there," Silas answered for her.

"He is?" Danielle said.

"Yes," Brianne confirmed and then turned to Silas. "How do you know?"

"He told me. He asked me to pray for you, and him."

"He did?"

"Yes, and he wanted me to know he's just doing it as a friend so that if word gets around and I hear about it another way, I wouldn't get the wrong idea."

"Austin is so sweet," Danielle said. "He didn't come across that way when I first met him, but the more I get to know him, the more I see it. He's like you, Silas, only—I don't know. What's the word?"

Brianne knew what she meant, and she spoke the words she would use to describe him. "Risky and unpredictable—but in a good way."

Silas laughed. "That's another way of saying I'm sweet but dull."

"No, you're not," she said. "You're different than Austin. But I like you both just the way you are."

"I'm glad you're not going alone," Danielle said, stepping over to give her a hug. "I've been in situations like that before. In fact, that's how I met Vince, and that was definitely a mistake. Any guy who thinks it's fine to date a girl without her parents knowing about it is Trouble with a capital T. Remember that, Brianne."

"I will."

"I hope you have fun," Danielle said.

"Yeah, me too."

Silas and Danielle stepped away, and she told them both good-bye for now. Checking the mail in her hands as she headed for the house, she saw a letter from Sarah among the pile, although it looked more like a greeting card envelope, and she was right. Sarah had sent her a 'Thinking of You' card, and inside she'd written a short note that said, *I'll be praying for you tonight. No matter what happens, remember Jesus is with you. He will keep you safe and find ways to make you smile.*

Since she didn't have to be at Ashlee's until after dinner, she went to her room and did her homework so she wouldn't have to do it on Sunday afternoon, and then she decided to write a letter to Joel. She wanted to write to Sarah too, but she wanted to wait until she could tell her what happened tonight. But she wrote to Joel because no matter what happened at the movie theater, she wanted to let him know she had been doing what he said about not keeping her friends at a distance simply because she was afraid of having to say good-bye to them at some point.

When we lived in Sweet Home, I took full advantage of your friendship because the possibility of us moving never occurred to me, and now even though we have to go months without seeing each other, we're still close. I hold you close to my heart always, and whenever I do see you, it's pure joy for me. And it's the same way with Sarah because I never held back with her either. She never gave me that option. And I believe if I give everything to the friendships I have now, the result will be the same no matter where God takes me from here.

Thanks so much for challenging me in that because if you hadn't, I think I'd be going all alone tonight and be scared out of my mind, or not going at all, but right now I'm excited about spending two hours at the movies with Austin, and no matter what else happens tonight, I know that joy will carry me through.

I told Austin today he's a gift from God to me, and so are you, Joel. I love writing to you, even if you don't write back, but I'm glad you have been lately. I miss you.

Love,
Brianne

Chapter Fourteen

Brianne scanned the pictures in the booklet in her hands, trying to decide what "look" she wanted for her makeover. There were eight girls in their group, and only three girls could be worked on at a time, so while she was waiting for her turn, she was supposed to pick out the face and hair-look she was going for and the clothing style she wanted for the pictures.

She didn't really know the other girls, and they were helping each other decide and saying, 'Oh, that would be perfect for you!' or 'Yuck, who would ever pick that?' But Brianne preferred to make her own decision, and she sat quietly, trying to determine which look would be best for her.

Some of the choices were wild and completely unnatural that she discarded immediately. Others were sophisticated, sexy, or on-the-edge that seemed appealing at first, but she couldn't picture herself looking that way and feeling good about it, and then there were simple looks that reminded her of the way she looked normally with a few enhancements. Those choices were at the bottom, down in the corner, but that's what she wanted.

Because Ashlee had been one of the first to go and Brianne didn't know the other girls well, she read the book she had brought along while she waited. After the stylists finished with Ashlee and Caitlin and Jillene, they went to have their pictures taken while three more girls got fixed-up. She and a girl named Tara would be the last to go, and when it was just the two of them sitting there, Brianne closed her book and talked to Tara. They had math together, so she sort of knew her. But she hadn't known Tara was such a close friend of Ashlee's.

There were two elementary schools that fed into Clatskanie Junior High, and she knew Tara had either gone to the other one or to a private school, been homeschooled before this year, or had moved here this summer, but she realized she'd never asked her, so she did and learned she had gone to the other public school and lived in a small community in that area.

"How do you know Ashlee?"

"She's my lab partner in science, and we're also in the same P.E. class this semester. How do you know her?"

"She was in my fifth grade class, and I had several classes with her last year, and she goes to my church."

"What church do you go to?"

"Rivergate Community."

"We go to a really small church in Mist," she said. "Actually, my dad is the pastor there, but that's kind of embarrassing, so I don't tell people that."

"Why is it embarrassing?"

"I used to get made fun of a lot. Not so much now because I don't tell people."

"Does Ashlee know that?"

"Yes. But I swore her to secrecy. I'm not sure why I just told you," she laughed. "Don't tell anyone, okay?"

"My dad's a pastor too," she said, feeling very perplexed about why Tara was so embarrassed about it. She had never felt that way.

"He is?"

"Yes. That's why we moved here two years ago."

"Isn't it awful?"

"Not really," she said. "I've never felt that way about it."

"Well, I hate it."

Brianne didn't comment further and changed the subject, asking Tara what pictures she had marked on her card. Brianne thought she had made good choices and showed Tara her own selections.

"That's almost what you look like now," Tara said. "I like it, but don't you want to look different?"

"Not really," she said. "I'm not into this kind of stuff. But this is what Ashlee wanted to do, so I'm going along with it."

"Did you hear she invited a bunch of guys to the movie?" she asked, checking to make sure Ashlee's mom wasn't around when she said it.

"Yes, Ashlee told me yesterday. When did she tell you?"

"This morning. I don't have a boyfriend, so she's setting me up with someone. Is she doing that with you too?"

"No. I mean, she said she could because I don't have a boyfriend either, but I asked one of my friends, and he's going to be there."

Ashlee must have been the first to have her pictures taken because she returned and came to sit by them. She still had her wardrobe on, and she wanted to know what selections they had made and expressed her opinion of Tara's, getting her to change the makeup choice and add a hat to her accessories.

"Brianne, that's so simple," she said about her choices. "You already look like that. Try something different."

"I don't want to look different," she said. "This is me. This is what I want."

"Okay, whatever."

Ashlee went back to the photo-shoot room to watch the other girls, and Tara went to use the bathroom. While she was alone, Brianne decided to call her mom and dad, just to let them know she was fine so far, and then she called Austin too.

"Does she know I'm coming yet?" he asked.

"No. She hasn't asked."

"If you have to tell her, it's fine, but I hope she doesn't know until she sees me there."

"You're bad," she said. "This is not about you and your torment of Ashlee Moore."

"I know. It's all about you, and I plan to make it that way."

"What's that mean?"

"It means when I meet you at the theater, I'm going to pretend like Ashlee isn't even there. I refuse to give her the satisfaction of glaring at me from across the room."

"And if she completely ignores you?"

"All the better. Either way, I win."

"Well, whatever you do, I'm glad you're going to be there. And follow my lead because I'm going to try and sit by Tara—you know the girl who sits in front of you in math?"

"Yes."

"She's here, and Ashlee set her up with a guy, so I want us to watch out for her if possible."

"Okay."

"I have to go. See you in an hour."

She clicked off the phone and put it back into her purse as Tara returned, and within a few minutes they were being called back to get into the chairs for their makeovers. When Brianne pointed out her selections to the young woman, she smiled and said, "Perfect for you. Absolutely perfect."

The next thirty minutes were actually kind of fun. The woman who did her hair and makeup was funny and sweet, and she kept saying, 'Your skin is so light and smooth. What do you wash it with?' or 'What moisturizer do you use?' or a dozen other questions Brianne never seemed to have a satisfactory answer for except when she asked if she always used sunscreen, and she said, 'Most of the time when I go to the beach or the river, but not every day.'

"Well, use some every day, and I bet your skin will still be this way when you're thirty. But that's good you wear it at the beach and stuff."

And then with her hair it was, "Where do you get it highlighted? It's so perfect."

"I don't. This is all me."

"I thought it must be because it's so soft, but I've never seen such perfectly highlighted hair! I'm so serious. I've been doing this for five years, and I've never seen it."

"God makes us each unique," she said. "Why make us all look the same when He doesn't have to? That's what my dad always says."

"He's a smart man. You should listen to him."

"I usually do. He's a pastor, so I figure he knows what he's talking about most of the time."

"Smart and beautiful? He's going to be turning those boys away one of these days, or is he already?"

"No. I don't date yet. I want to wait until I'm sixteen."

"More power to you, honey. Boy, do I wish I would have done that. Eighteen or twenty would have been even better. Most guys are idiots until at least then. Even now I have a hard time finding a good one."

"How old are you? If you don't mind me asking."

"Twenty-eight. And to be honest, I'm a little tired of waiting for Prince Charming to show up."

"But you're so pretty. You must have a lot of guys asking you out."

"Guys asking me out, yes. Guys worth my time, no."

"You should try going to church. I have three guys who are good friends right now who I would go out with if I was older, and they all go to church."

"Hmm. Never thought of that," she said. "Maybe I'll give it a try. I certainly couldn't do any worse."

When she turned her so she could look in the mirror, Brianne was happy with what she saw. She didn't look all that different except her skin was a more even color, her eyes looked bigger, and her lips were a nice shade of icy pink.

"What do you think?"

"I like it," she said, running her fingers through her hair. The dark blonde strands were straight like usual, but it had more body to it and looked very shiny. "Thank you."

"You're welcome. You can go back there and get your wardrobe now. That lipstick should go perfectly with the pink top you chose."

Brianne headed back to the dressing room area, and another woman helped her find the right clothes and adjusted everything after she had them on. The picture-taking process was a little tedious because she was supposed to hold her head a certain way and look in the right spot and try to smile naturally while holding the pose that felt weird. But the proofs on the computer screen she got to see when they were finished looked okay. Tara had gone before her, so she was the last one, and then everyone was waiting for her after she got changed.

On the way to the movie theater she was sitting in the front seat of the minivan beside Ashlee's mom, and

Mrs. Moore asked her a lot of questions about school and church and how she had been doing with Sarah being gone. And then when they were about a minute from the theater, Mrs. Moore turned to speak to Ashlee who was sitting behind them.

"You know, Ash. I think I'll stay and see the movie with you. I'm tired and don't feel like driving all the way home."

"But I thought Daddy was picking us up? You should go home and rest, Mom. We'll be fine."

"Are you sure? It's going to be late by the time you get out. You're usually not out this late."

"We'll be inside the whole time, Mom. We'll be fine."

Brianne was amazed with Ashlee's ability to sound so calm about it, not letting a hint of anything slip, even though her plan could be greatly altered by this. *She must do this a lot.*

"Okay, Ash," she said, pulling into the parking lot. "But I want you all to stay inside afterwards until your dad gets here."

"We will," Ashlee said as if she would never do otherwise. "Don't be such a worrier, Mom. Nothing's going to happen. It's a perfectly safe public place."

Her mom pulled up to the front curb to let them all out. Brianne opened her door and said good-bye to Ashlee's mom and then followed the others to the ticket booth where Ashlee was paying for all of them. Ashlee's mom waited in the van until they had their tickets and were heading inside. Ashlee went back to the van to say good-bye to her through the passenger side window, and Brianne hung back as the others went inside.

Once her mom drove away, Ashlee came to meet her, and they walked side-by-side toward the door. "We're a little later than I said, so most of the guys are probably here," Ashlee said. "I told them to wait inside for us. The guy I set you up with is named Jordan. He's a friend of Kirk's who's on the swim team. He's a ninth grader too, but I think you'll really like him. They're so much more mature than seventh graders, and he's really cute."

"Oh, thanks, but I asked someone else to meet me here," she said, trying to sound casual about it but hearing the nervousness in her voice. Her heart was about to pound out of her chest. This was so not her thing!

"Brianne!" Ashlee said, sounding impressed. "Why didn't you tell me? Who is it? Silas?"

"No," she said, stepping ahead of Ashlee to hand her ticket to the person inside the door. Brianne scanned the lobby while she waited for Ashlee and saw Austin not more than ten feet away. He had already seen her and was walking toward them.

She smiled at him but waited for him to come to her. Ashlee came up from behind and spoke before Austin made it all the way.

"Then who, Brianne Carmichael? I can't believe you didn't tell—"

Her voice stopped, and Brianne didn't have to look at Ashlee to know she had caught sight of Austin.

Austin didn't look at Ashlee or acknowledge her presence in the least. His eyes were directly focused on her, and the first words out of his mouth were, "You're late, but it's worth it. Wow! You look amazing."

Chapter Fifteen

"Thanks," Brianne replied to Austin's compliment. "It was fun."

"Austin Lockhart!" Ashlee interrupted. "What are you doing here?"

Austin looked at Ashlee then, as if he'd just noticed her standing there. "Brianne invited me. She was supposed to, wasn't she?"

"Yes, but—. Brianne!" she said in a hushed voice, as if she didn't want Austin to hear. "You weren't supposed to invite him!"

"Why not?"

"Because he's not a guy!"

Brianne laughed. "He's not?"

"I mean—. Never mind, I can't believe you did this to me. I'm never speaking to you again!"

Ashlee marched off, and Brianne waited a moment before looking at Austin because she knew as soon as she did, she would start laughing.

"Wow. I guess she really does hate you, doesn't she?"

Austin met her gaze and smiled. "See how she gets when you don't play by her rules?"

Brianne was tempted to watch Ashlee as she went to join the other girls and find her date, but remembering what Austin had said on the phone earlier, she decided to focus on him for now. She felt so glad he was here, especially after hearing Ashlee had planned to set her up with a ninth-grader. She would be absolutely dying right now if she had ended up in that situation.

"I'm really glad you're here," she said, reaching for his hand and giving it a gentle squeeze. "On the way in, Ashlee told me she set me up with some guy who's fifteen."

Austin smiled. "I'm glad I'm here too. Do you want some popcorn?"

"Sure," she said, releasing his hand and walking beside him to the snack bar. Glancing at Ashlee and her mob, she could tell they were discussing something, and she had a feeling Ashlee was upset Austin was here because now they couldn't go someplace else without her youth pastor's son knowing about it, and Ashlee knew Austin wouldn't hesitate for a second to tattle on her.

They got popcorn, a drink to share, and red licorice—which was Brianne's favorite candy and Austin's too, as they had discovered the first time they'd come to the movies together. They decided to go into the theater and not wait to see what the rest of the group did. Austin had them sit in the very back so they could see Ashlee and everyone else when they came in—if they ever did. Brianne had already decided if they didn't, she was going home with Austin after this, and depending on how Ashlee treated her, she might anyway.

The whole clan did come in about fifteen minutes later, after the previews had started but not the movie. Most of them had to spread out and find whatever seats were available. She had forgotten about wanting to try and sit by Tara, but if they had waited until now to come in, she probably wouldn't have been able to anyway. She was glad Austin had thought ahead to have them sit in the top row because she knew where all the different couples were, and she could see plainly if any of them left and were gone for a significant amount of time.

She wasn't sure what she would do if that happened, but somehow she knew Austin had some kind of plan. "How do you know so much about the right way to handle difficult situations?" she asked.

"What do you mean?"

"Like this—tonight," she whispered. "This was all your idea, and it's working out perfectly. If I had tried to handle it myself, I'd be sitting there with that guy right now."

"I don't know," he shrugged. "It just made the most sense to me. Someone has a plan I don't like—I make up a different one. Ashlee's not God, Brianne. It's okay to mess with her ideas."

"I can't believe she said you're not a guy. Who did she expect me to invite? Brady?"

"I don't think she expected you to invite anybody. This isn't about you. It's about her. You show up tonight with nobody, and she has someone waiting to save the day. She wants you to be her friend, Brianne, but she doesn't know how to do that."

"But she doesn't have to do anything. I already am—but I might not be much longer if she keeps trying to pull stuff like this."

"You remember that. Remember she should be trying to earn your friendship, not the other way around."

The movie was starting, so they stopped talking, but Brianne thought about his words. She knew in the past she had tried to earn Ashlee's friendship, but she wasn't sure why, and she had done very little to earn Austin's, and yet here he was, being the exact friend she needed him to be.

And Austin had definitely earned her friendship. He was a real friend, and she felt so thankful for him. If she needed something, he would be there, and he would never try to pull her into something she didn't want to be a part of or expect her to be someone she wasn't.

A couple of times during the movie, Brianne wanted to lay her head against Austin's shoulder or reach for his hand. Even if this wasn't a date, it felt like it more than the other times they'd spent together. But she didn't do either. Imagining it and actually doing it were two different things, and she wasn't ready for that with Austin or anyone.

When the movie ended they made their way back to the lobby, and Brianne wasn't sure what she was going to do. All of the guys either left or went to the video game area, and Ashlee and the other girls went to stand by the door and wait for Mr. Moore to arrive. Brianne stepped over to see if Ashlee was still speaking to her, and when she didn't, she decided to tell her she was going home with Austin.

"You can't do that!" Ashlee spouted.

"Why not?"

"What am I supposed to tell my mom and dad?"

"I don't know. The truth?"

Ashlee's eyes flashed with anger, and she turned away. Brianne had her gift in her purse, so she took out the small package and handed it to her.

"Happy Birthday, Ashlee. Thanks for inviting me. The makeover thing was fun."

Ashlee took the gift but didn't say anything.

"Are you going to be at the babysitting thing tomorrow?"

"What do you think?"

"We'll be getting some good money for camp."

"Yeah, like I'm going after what you did tonight."

"I don't want you to go for me. I want you to go for you."

Ashlee ignored her. She stepped away without saying anything else and met Austin by the door. Brianne felt close to tears, but she didn't let them fall until they were outside and heading for his dad's truck. She knew she needed to show Ashlee tough love right now and let her know the way she was living was wrong, but it was hard for her to be that way. She would rather keep trying to be a friend by pleasing Ashlee, but that way wasn't working, and she knew it.

Austin put his arm around her shoulder and pulled her close to him. "You're doing the right thing," he said. "I'm very proud of you."

She didn't respond, and she didn't say much for the next ten minutes. Pastor Doug didn't ask what happened, but he knew she was upset. And it occurred to her on the way home that Austin was very much like his dad. Pastor Doug might not be a young and flashy type of youth pastor, but he knew what was going on, and he cared.

"You know, Brianne, I start praying for you kids way before you ever come into the youth group. I've known Ashlee since she was a baby, and I've been praying for her for a long time. She's always had that rebellious streak that's going to be tough to break, but I've been praying, and I believe God will bring her around, and you know one of the primary ways I think He's going to work?"

"How?"

"Through you."

"Why do you think that?"

"Because you have the heart for it. You're the only person I've ever known who has cried over her."

Ashlee had made her cry many times before, but usually because she had hurt her in some way. But tonight she wasn't crying for herself and her pain, she was crying for Ashlee.

She laughed. "What's the matter with me? Who cries over someone like Ashlee Moore?"

"A real friend, that's who; and like it or not, that's you."

Brianne didn't say anything else. There wasn't anything to say. She had no idea how she was going to be Ashlee's friend after this, but she decided she didn't have to try and figure it out. Somehow God would lead her, and He would provide whatever she needed. Tonight she had needed Austin and his plan, and next time she might need something completely different, but she knew one thing for sure—she couldn't figure it out for herself, and that was okay.

When they arrived at the house, Austin walked her up to the front door. She turned to face him and thanked him again for being there tonight, and for his friendship.

"Since Ashlee's not your best friend anymore, I figure someone has to be."

She smiled. "I suppose you will do."

"You're a special person, Brianne. The more time I spend with you, the more I see that. I always thought you were nice, but what my dad said is true. You go beyond nice to really loving people."

"Yeah, look who's talking?"

"I ain't crying any tears over Ashlee."

"Maybe not, but there are others I know you would: Michael, your family, me."

"And don't forget Sarah. I cried major tears over her."

She laughed. "I'm serious."

"Me too. She's very pretty, you know."

Brianne folded her arms in front of her chest and gave him a fake glare. He tousled her hair.

"Hey," she said, ducking away from him. "You're messing up my perfect hair."

"So? You're still beautiful."

The front door opened, and her dad interrupted. He seemed happy to see her.

"Hi, Dad," she said, stepping into his arms. "I decided to come home."

"Good night, Brianne," Austin said. "I'll see you tomorrow."

"Okay. Thanks. And tell your dad thanks too—for bringing me home, and the other stuff."

"Me too," her dad said, stepping onto the porch to shake Austin's hand and wave at his dad. "You're a good man, Austin. I appreciate it."

"Not a problem, Pastor Jake. See you Sunday."

Austin stepped away, and her dad followed her inside. The house was quiet, and Brianne hadn't thought until now about how late it was. She had also forgotten about her appearance until her dad saw her in the full light and got a very interesting look on his face: sort of a cross between a smile and having chest pains.

He didn't comment on it, but he had them sit down, and she told him everything that was of any importance to him, leaving out some of the girl-drama for his sake and hers.

The phone rang at nearly midnight, just as Brianne had finished telling him about leaving with Austin and what Pastor Doug had told her on the way home. Brianne could tell by her dad's response to the caller it was Ashlee's mom calling to make sure she was there.

"Yeah, she's here," he said. "But she's not sick. She wanted to come home because she and Ashlee had a bit of a fight."

Her dad paused while Mrs. Moore said something, and then he responded. "No, I believe it had something to do with who Brianne chose to invite to the movies. Ashlee wanted to set her up with someone else, but Brianne wanted to bring her own date."

More silence.

"No, Brianne was quite clear. You didn't know about the guys who were meeting the girls there?"

Brianne had been wondering if her parents would end up confronting Ashlee's mom and dad with the truth about her secret plans for tonight, and she knew Ashlee had just been caught by her own lie. Ashlee had lied about why she had left, but her dad wasn't going to lie to confirm her story. He hadn't interfered until he didn't have any other choice.

Brianne could hear her dad's role change from parent-to-parent with Mrs. Moore, to pastor-to-member of his church, and Brianne didn't feel it was appropriate to keep listening, so she went to wash her face and get ready for bed.

Looking at herself in the mirror before she turned on the water and reached for her face cleanser, she liked the way she looked, except for the smudges under her eyes from crying earlier, but she didn't want to look like this every day. For one thing, it would take way too much work to put on that much makeup in the morning, and she would get tired of it really fast. And for another thing, it made her look like she was sixteen, and she wasn't. She was thirteen, and that was fine with her.

She wouldn't feel right being around Austin and her other real friends looking like this. She would feel like she wasn't being herself. She would feel out of place and like she was trying to impress her friends who she didn't need to impress with how she looked. They liked her for who she was, and she liked them back in the same way.

Going to say good night to her dad after she had done everything except get into her pajamas, she saw he was off the phone, but it had been a difficult call for him. She decided not to ask him about it and sat on his lap to give him a hug.

"I love you, Daddy. Thanks for waiting up for me."

"I love you, sweetheart."

"Do you think I did the right thing? Ashlee said she's not going to camp now."

"Why did you decide to come home?"

"I'm not sure. It just felt right," she said. "Austin said something about how I can't earn Ashlee's friendship—at least not on her terms, and I knew that if I went back to the house after what she said to me, that's pretty much what I'd be doing."

"Austin's smart for only being thirteen."

"I think he gets it from his dad. He listens to people and watches them and sees below the surface. And he's had Ashlee figured out since they were three."

Her dad smiled. "And how about you? Does he have you figured out?"

"He knows me better than I do."

"But in your case, he likes what he knows?"

"I guess so. He keeps hanging around."

Her dad smiled and kissed her on the forehead. "Like I said, he's a smart kid."

"Good night, Daddy."

"Good night, sweetheart. I love you."

Chapter Sixteen

On Saturday Brianne received a letter from her cousin Justine saying she had sent in the registration form for camp but Jenna was still thinking about it. Justine also thanked her for the devotional book and said she had already started and really liked it so far.

Brianne also got a phone call from Sarah. She needed to tell her about the details of their trip to Lake Tahoe that was only a week away. Sarah and her mom would be coming to pick her up next Sunday afternoon, their plane would be leaving from Portland early Monday morning, they would fly back Friday, and bring her home on Saturday. Sarah said the weather there this time of year could be anything from warm and sunny to snowing and freezing cold, so she would need to pack a good variety of clothing, but she told her to definitely bring her bathing suit because the resort had an indoor pool.

"Bring something nice too," she said. "We'll probably eat at the fancy restaurant there."

"Okay. I can't wait. This is going to be so fun."

"I know. So, how did things go last night?"

"Good," she said. "From my perspective anyway." She told her all the details, and Sarah said the same thing Austin had.

"You did the right thing. I'm proud of you."

"I never could have done that without Austin, and with all those prayers I know you said for me."

"That's what friends are for," she said.

"Do you think I should try to talk to Ashlee, or leave her alone?"

"Wait for the right moments. You'll know when they come."

Brianne remembered Sarah's advice the following morning when she saw Ashlee at church. She was sort of surprised she was there but had the feeling she had been forced to come. Ashlee didn't look at her, but her behavior couldn't take away from the joy of the morning for Brianne.

Marissa hadn't wanted to get baptized until her parents were okay with it and agreed to come, and they were there to see both her and Miguel get baptized during the morning church service. Some of Marissa's friends who had been coming to youth group, and Miguel's girlfriend, Andrea, were there also.

Brianne was sitting beside Austin and his family, and Silas and Danielle were on the other side of her, and all four of them had tears in their eyes along with their smiles as Pastor Doug asked Marissa and Miguel to proclaim their faith in Jesus and then put them under the water and lifted them back up as a symbol of their new life in Christ.

Brianne thought her dad's message was particularly good as he shared about the difference knowing Jesus should make in their lives. "In Colossians 3:12-15, it says because God loves us we should be tenderhearted and kind, humble and gentle, patient and forgiving, and the most important thing is to love others. This will bring peace and unity. Isn't that what we all want? How many of you enjoy conflict? How many of you just wake up every day hoping you can have a good fight with someone and be miserable? No. That's not what we want. We want peace and joy and harmony, and we can have that with Jesus when we let Him control us and we live the way He says is best."

Brianne had been wondering what she was supposed to do now that Ashlee wasn't speaking to her, and the truth from the Bible gave her the answer: She needed to stay close to Jesus. Only He could give her a loving heart for Ashlee. Only God could give her the patience to be a friend to someone who didn't want friends that didn't play by her rules.

One of the traditions her dad had started here at the church was to have a special catered lunch after church for those who had been baptized and their families, and close friends were invited to stay also. Her mom and dad always hosted it, and Brianne and her siblings always stayed, but this time Brianne got to sit at the place of honor beside Marissa, the place usually reserved for the person who had been the greatest spiritual influence in that person's life.

Miguel considered his sister to be that person for him, along with Pastor Doug, and Marissa and Miguel had invited everyone in the youth group to stay. The whole crowd filled up several tables, and Brianne really enjoyed being a part of seeing two people she had been praying for experiencing new life in the reality of God's love for them.

From where she was sitting, Brianne could look out the window and see the new youth building under construction, and she had a vision of a lot of good things happening there in the future. But she also knew she didn't have to wait for a new building to make a difference in the lives of her friends and classmates. Just by being Marissa's friend for two years, she had been given the opportunity to help her to know God in a personal way, and then Marissa had done that for Miguel by praying for him and being a good sister even though he had been having some problems and hadn't always been the best brother to her.

Ashlee hadn't stayed for lunch, and Brianne knew it wasn't going to be easy, but she wasn't going to stop praying for Ashlee to make her life different than it was now. The sad part for Brianne was that unlike Marissa, who hadn't known God because no one had ever told her about Him, Ashlee did know Him, but she wasn't living like it. She was making bad choices that could get her into some serious trouble one of these days, and she also seemed very unhappy most of the time. She acted like she was fine: having fun, dating boys, being the leader of a popular circle of friends; and yet she got very upset when things didn't go her way, she felt the need to lie to her parents, and she pushed away the friendships of those who really cared about her.

Brianne couldn't imagine living that way, but she also knew she could end up there if she allowed people like Ashlee to control her decisions instead of going to people God had placed in her life she could trust: Her parents, good friends like Sarah and Austin, and Pastor Doug. She knew Friday night would have turned out much differently if she had tried to handle it all herself, lied to her parents, and not prayed about it.

But she had asked God for help and taken the advice of others worth listening to. Ashlee wasn't speaking to her right now, but she knew she had done the right thing and that God would work it out somehow. He had taken care of her so far, and if she didn't believe Jesus would continue to do that, she couldn't believe in anything about Him.

After lunch Austin and his brother came over to her house to play video games with her brothers, as they often did on Sunday afternoons. Beth's birthday was coming up on Tuesday, and her mom and dad needed to go to Longview to pick up her present: an outdoor playhouse. They left her in charge while they were gone, but Beth was napping so there wasn't anything to do except watch the boys play video games.

Her brothers usually got along well when they played because if they didn't, then her parents would take away the privilege for a couple of days. But when Austin was there, they were always on their best behavior because he and Calvin would often bring games her brothers didn't have, and he was good about helping them get along and making sure everyone had a turn and played fairly.

When she could see her presence wasn't really needed, she went out onto the porch to pet her cats and write a letter to Sarah. She had talked to her yesterday and told her about Friday night, but she shared a few more personal things about how she had felt being around those other girls and the sharp contrast she felt between that and her time with Austin. She also told her about Marissa and Miguel getting baptized, and she asked her to pray for the rest of Marissa's family, Miguel's girlfriend, and Marissa's friends who had been there this morning.

Hearing the door open behind her as she was finishing up the letter, she turned and saw Austin coming out of the house. He sat beside her and asked her something she had forgotten about.

"So what's your mom and dad's story?"

She told him everything she knew and was a little surprised at the primary thing that stood out to him.

"Your mom never kissed a guy until she was twenty?"

"That's what she says."

"Huh," he said, as if he was pondering something.

"What?"

"Is that what you're planning to do?"

"I don't know. I don't think my mom planned it. She just never felt right about kissing anyone until she met my dad."

"Have you ever kissed anybody?"

She laughed. "No. Have you?"

152

"No."

"And since I'm planning to wait until I'm sixteen to date, I think I'll wait until at least then to kiss someone."

"Why?"

"Why?"

"Yeah. Why do you want to wait?"

She thought for a moment. "I guess because it's a special thing, and I don't want to be kissing anyone just because he wants to kiss me, or because I think he's cute. I want it to mean something."

"Make him ask permission first."

"Who?"

"Whoever you decide you want to kiss. My dad told me if I want to kiss a girl, I should ask permission first."

Okay, Austin Lockhart. I'll make sure you ask me first.

She smiled at her private thoughts, but she didn't even think of giving them away. Instead she asked him something she had forgotten about until now.

"What are you afraid of?"

"Huh?"

"On Thursday night you told me you were afraid of this—whatever it is that's happening with us."

He smiled. "Ah, yes. You wanted my top five fears."

"Yes, but then I forgot to ask you on Friday."

He numbered them off one-by-one on his fingers without having to think about it. "Going too fast and making a complete mess of it; going too slow and losing you to someone else; falling in love with you and then you breaking my heart; you falling in love with me and then I break your heart; and, we fall in love with each other, it's perfect, and we live happily ever after."

Brianne felt shocked he had given it serious thought. "Why does the last one scare you?"

"Because you've known me since you were ten, and you're going to have so many stories to tell our kids about what an idiot I was, especially the fact I liked your best friend in sixth grade instead of you."

She laughed. "That will give me something to tell our daughter when the boy she likes, likes someone else. I'll say, 'Just wait a year, honey. You never know. He might change his mind.'"

"Or, 'Someone better will come along'?"

"Not necessarily better, maybe just different. The right one for her."

"Is that what your mom told you when you were crying your eyes out over me last year?"

She gave him a good shove and laughed. "I never cried over you, Austin Lockhart. Keep dreaming."

Chapter Seventeen

Austin smiled but didn't say anything else. She wasn't sure if he was teasing her or what, but she decided to be honest about her fears too.

"Do you know what scares me the most?"

"What?"

"Losing your friendship, for whatever reason. I don't want that to happen, okay? Even if you start dating someone else when we're sixteen, or I do, or we date each other and then break up. Promise me we'll always be friends?"

"Even if you move away?" he asked.

"Yes."

"Do you think we can really do that?"

"Yes. Me and Sarah are still friends, aren't we?"

"Yeah, but she's a girl."

"Me and Joel are still friends."

"If I ask you something, will you give me an honest answer?"

"Yes."

"Do you like Joel—I mean, do you think he could ever be more than a friend?"

Six months ago she would have said no to that. But with her current feelings for Austin she never thought she would have, she knew anything was possible, and having either Austin or Joel for a boyfriend—she could certainly do a lot worse.

"At this point I'm not hoping for it, but I'm not going to say it could never happen."

Austin didn't say anything.

"Does that bother you?"

"Yes."

She laughed. She knew he was being serious but sort of teasing her at the same time.

"See? This is why I don't want to date now. I don't know *who* or *what* I want. You're my friend, Austin. And so is Joel, and so is Silas. I don't want to be anyone's girlfriend right now. I'm thirteen!"

"But if you had to pick now, you'd pick me, right?"

She smiled at him. "Now? You're the only one here."

"If I asked for permission to kiss you, what would you say?"

"Are you asking?" she challenged him.

"No."

"Why not?"

"Because I know you'll say no."

"You're right."

"Would you say no to Silas?"

"Yes."

"Would you say no to Joel?"

She laughed. She had a hard time imagining Joel ever asking her that, now or ever. But if he did, she would have the hardest time saying no to him. He would never ask her something like that unless he really wanted it and had a reason to believe she would say yes.

"Would you?" Austin asked again.

"I can't imagine that. Not right now. That's not Joel."

Austin changed the subject. "Are you excited about the band trip?"

At the end of the month, the weekend after Spring Break, their band was going on a two-day trip to Eugene and Newport.

"I'm excited about having time with three of my best friends," she answered, "plus some others too."

"Does that mean I have to hang around with a bunch of girls?"

"No, but I think it would be fun. Marissa and Brooke like you. They think you're 'all right' for a boy."

"Do you wish it was Brooke, Marissa, and Sarah you would be hanging out with instead of Brooke, Marissa, and me?"

"No."

"Liar."

She laughed. "I'm not lying. Me and Sarah are better when it's just the two of us, but with you it doesn't matter if it's just us, or we're with a group. It's the same."

He seemed to accept that, and she knew it was the honest truth even though she really hadn't thought about it until now. She looked at her watch and knew Beth might be waking up soon. She told Austin she needed to go check on her, and he followed her inside. She went to her room and seeing Beth still sound asleep, she went out to the living room and sat beside Austin on the couch.

"When are you getting your pictures back?" he asked.

"Sometime this week," she said. "If Ashlee gives me mine."

"How many are you getting?"

"We get a proof sheet of all the photos, and I can select one and get some free five-by-sevens and wallets of that one, and then if we want more we can order them, but we have to pay for those."

"Do I get one?"

She laughed. "You have my school picture from this year, and you see me every day. What do you need another picture of me for?"

"Is Joel getting one?"

"I haven't decided who's getting any."

"But you've thought about it."

Brianne didn't know how he knew that, but he was right. And yes, she had thought of sending one to Joel, and to Sarah, but she hadn't thought of giving one to Austin or Silas or any of her other friends here. That seemed weird. They saw her all the time.

Her mom and dad stepped through the door before she had a chance to respond, and after her dad caught sight of them sitting there on the couch together and gave Austin a look that made Brianne laugh, she leaned over and whispered something in Austin's ear.

"Right now the only boy I'm giving one of those pictures to is my daddy."

"What are you whispering over there?" her dad said.

Brianne got up from the couch and followed her mom and dad into the kitchen to help with putting the groceries away they had brought home. After her dad set the bags on the counter, she stepped close to give him a hug, and he squeezed her gently in return.

"Everything go all right here?"

She laughed. "Fine, Daddy."

"Your mom said it was okay to leave you here, but I wasn't so sure."

"You've told me you trust Austin. Has he done anything to change that?"

"No, but I'd appreciate it if you didn't whisper secrets to him when I'm in the room. It makes me nervous."

"I was just telling him who the most special guy in my life is."

"Okay, never mind," he laughed. "I don't want to hear that kind of information."

"Oh, I think you do, Jacob," her mom interrupted, tossing her a wink.

"You should listen to your wife, Daddy."

"All right. Who is he?"

"Who do you think it is?"

"I wouldn't even want to guess." He started taking things out of the bags in front of him and handing them to her. Brianne stepped away to put the cereal in the cupboard.

"It should be obvious, Jacob," her mom said. "Go ahead, take a guess."

"Austin," he said.

"No," Brianne answered, coming to take the packages of spaghetti from him.

"Joel?"

She laughed. "No."

"Some guy I've never heard of?"

"No, Daddy. It's you."

She stepped away to put the spaghetti in its place, and when she returned, he gave her another hug but this one lasted longer.

"I love you too, sweetheart, but I know someday there is going to be a boy who becomes a very special part of your heart, and I want to make sure it's someone who's worthy of you. That's my job."

Brianne saw her dad a bit differently than she ever had before. She had always seen him as *being* her dad, but not so much as him having to *be* her dad. All the prayers he had prayed for her, all the fears he had about difficult moments she might face or bad choices she could make, all the love he had given he had no guarantee she would ever return, all the ways he provided for her and made her life so much easier than it could be.

"I love you, Daddy. Keep reminding me you know more about life and boys than I do, and I'll do my best to listen, okay?"

"Okay. And listen to your heart too, Brianne. God is there, and He knows even more than I do."

Brianne kept thinking about her dad's words off and on for the rest of the day: when Austin said something about having a fun afternoon with her;

when Silas came by that evening to bring back movies his family had borrowed; and when she went to bed and reread her most recent letter from Joel she had been keeping in her Bible.

Trying to determine what her heart was telling her about the different boys in her life, she honestly didn't know. Like she had told Austin, she didn't think she could know that yet. Yes, she liked them all for different reasons, and the thought of having a boyfriend seemed exciting and fun. But she knew she wasn't ready. If she chose one over the others now, it could be disastrous. She could be trading three perfectly good friendships for a few weeks or months of a different kind of relationship with one of them that might not work out, and then where would she be? Left with three so-so friendships that were awkward and confusing. It wasn't worth it at this point.

But she also knew someday one of them, or someone she hadn't met yet, would stand out to her above the others, and she would enter into a different kind of relationship with a boy than she ever had before. Her dad had said to listen to her heart, and she supposed he knew what he was talking about, but right now it seemed complicated and scary.

What if she made the wrong choice? What if by the time she was sixteen, Austin, Silas, Joel, and all the other guys she knew were looking elsewhere, and she ended up with no one who felt special about her?

What if girls like Ashlee really did win in the game of love, having all these fun and great times while she sat alone on Friday nights with nothing but her unrealistic ideals about the kind of boyfriend and relationship she wanted but would never find?

A familiar verse came to mind, but she wasn't sure why. It didn't seem to be anything that related to her current thoughts.

"Do not let your hearts be troubled. Trust in God, trust also in me. In my Father's house are many rooms; if it were not so I would have told you. I am going there to prepare a place for you."

But she kept thinking about it, and the words, 'prepare a place' stood out to her, and she wondered if Jesus wasn't just talking about Heaven, but places here on earth too—moments and events and blessings God already had all planned out for her. Perfect places she had to follow Him to find.

He seemed to answer her thoughts. *Do not let your heart be troubled, Brianne. I know the way I have prepared for you. If there was no hope, I'd just say so, but there is! I have so many wonderful plans for you. Just trust Me, and I'll get you there. I promise.*

I love to hear from my readers

Write me at:

living_loved@yahoo.com

25853949R00094